THE XENO MANIFESTO
REDEMPTION

BRYSEN MANN

Time Matters Publishing
www.brysenmann.com

ISBN
978-1-7753639-2-7 (Paperback)
978-1-7753639-3-4 (eBook)

DEDICATION

To all those who have taken the time
to read my saga, giving me the opportunity to try and right a wrong…
The Xeno Manifesto trilogy.

ACKNOWLEDGEMENTS

To those who strive to make a positive difference in this world. I thank you and wish you the best.

PROLOGUE

Felix Belette, the Weasel, the Appointed Representative…AR for short, for the Committee, doesn't normally watch TV. He despises it in fact but today he's glued to the set, ever since the story broke around nine this morning. He isn't happy as the events unfold and his anger and frustration only grows as the day wears on and more details are revealed. "You stupid cock suckers!" He yells at the big screen as he throws yet another half full whiskey glass of bourbon against the wall, glass shattering everywhere. Broken shards crunch under his brown and cognac handmade oxfords from the half dozen he's destroyed so far as he paces the floor, maneuvering around his beloved custom made leather office chair now lying on its side that he sent flying earlier. His tan designer suit jacket lies in a crumpled ball in a corner, the same place he tossed it and his white shirt sleeves are rolled up baring thin white hairless forearms, his shirt collar is unbuttoned and his brown paisley tie is loose, flung back over his shoulder. He's been cursing the TV constantly and had already warned his assistant not to intrude no matter what he hears coming from Felix's office. "Christ! It wasn't that complicated you son of a bitches!" He shouts as he grabs his small head with both hands, his bony fingers interlacing with his thinning greasy grey hair, yanking, as if he's trying to dislodge it from his body. He lets go, shaking it in bewilderment and stomps to the window facing the expansive mansion grounds sprawled before him. He violently yanks one side of the tied back, heavy red velvet drapes, dislodging them along with the elaborate gold gilded rod from its mounts and everything comes crashing down to the dark hardwood floor. He drops his head, rubbing his bloodshot eyes and pocked forehead, still in disbelief. He knows the Committee can't be pleased… he sure as fuck isn't.

"Mr. Belette?" His assistant calls out meekly from the office door.

Felix turns and there's no mistaking the look of rage on his face. "Mother fucker! What did I tell you, you…piece of shit! Get the hell out of here!" He screams in a high pitched voice sounding like a deranged lunatic.

"Mr. Belette?" His assistant squeaks out.

"Listen, you little son of a bitch I'm going to," Felix utters as he moves towards him.

"Ms. Kinsey is here!" His assistant yells out, a look of fright clearly expressed on his face.

Felix stops in his tracks. "Shit." He mutters as he scans around the room surveying the damage he's created.

"Give me a minute." Felix says.

"There is no minute." Olivia Kinsey states as she pushes past and tromps in, her heels clattering loudly on the low sheen wood floor. "Get out" She orders the assistant and he quickly exits unintentionally slamming the door closed behind him from the fear induced adrenalin rush in his system. Olivia Rosalind Kinsey gives Felix a vexed look from cold eyes as she stands there dressed in a pastel blue Ora floral embroidered silk-organza gown embellished with multi-colored floral embroidery with a wide ruffled hem. She has Saint Laurent Amber-metallic shoes on her feet and one hand holds a Roksanda round pebbled leather pouch. Her snow white hair is tied back in a tight ballet bun. Her skin is deathly pale but smooth and one would not realize she's well past eighty years old, the longest serving board member of the Committee, its matriarch.

"Olivia, it's not my fucking fault! I had this planned to perfection! It was the Goddamn operatives that screwed up!" Felix pleads as if he were a child.

Olivia approaches, looking him straight in the eye, she's a petite woman but the Weasel is short on stature himself. "How many times have I told you I do not appreciate foul language? Talk like that does not reflect the type of man the Committee expects of someone in your position and…how much have you had to drink? You reek of alcohol and you look like…a disheveled tramp."

"Fine, fine." Felix answers exasperated as he covers his mouth, stepping back, a pouty look on his face as he pulls his tie back around attempting to look as sober as possible. "Yes, I've had a few but nothing that will impair my judgment and…how do you want me to react? I mean, they barely got half the job done.

They missed the primary target at the Pentagon and didn't even make it to Pennsylvania Avenue?

"To be frank, I didn't agree with this strategy in the first place. But I was out voted." Olivia hisses out.

Felix is surprised by her comment. He was given the impression that all the Committee board members were behind him one hundred percent on this effort. "So now you've come to gloat, why else would you of all the board members be here?" He asks.

"I'm not petty. I'm here because this cannot be discussed over the phone no matter how secure the line may be. Now…it's all about damage control and ensuring nothing can come back to us here in the States."

"On us…or do you mean me?

"It's all the same at this juncture." Olivia states as she gives him a dubious look. "Our primary concern is that everyone we took extreme measures to carefully position after the fact, to fill the voids left and work on the behalf of the Committee, will not be proceeding. We need to step back now so we don't look over aggressive and raise suspicion. We'll have to work in the remaining balance of our people through other means."

"Don't give me that patronizing look Olivia. It was not my idea to source out the work to our Middle Eastern associates. I'm the one who wanted it all in-house…here, so we had better control, remember that." Felix spits out.

Olivia comes in close and jabs Felix hard in the chest with her index finger and he winces in pain as her pointed sky blue manicured finger nail makes contact. "You…better remember who you're talking to. Don't forget who I am and what I'm capable of; just try biting the hand that feeds you, you won't like where you end up." Olivia warns.

"I'm sorry." Felix says apologetically as he looks back at the screen, extending his arm towards it. "But how do you expect me to behave? I spent two years meticulously planning this and for what? Look at the shambles they…they have made of everything."

"Felix, it is what it is. We had no choice but to have others involved. We could not have this come back on us here in any way if it failed…like it just did. There were no guarantees the outcome would have been different no matter who we used. It was a complicated plan…maybe too complicated."

Felix wants to snap at her for that comment but holds back. Regardless of his seniority and position, she can take him down in a heartbeat.

"So you're here for what reason again?" He asks sarcastically, glaring at her.

Olivia stares him down and Felix finally looks away. "I'm here to tell you in person and on behalf of the entire Committee, to clean this all up. Make sure there is nothing…absolutely nothing that can come back to haunt us on this. You hear me? I want you to personally go through everything with a fine tooth comb. You planned this; you knew the rewards if it succeeded…and the consequences if it failed. Understood?"

Felix sighs heavily as he sheepishly looks at her. "I understand." He answers meekly.

Olivia heads for the door stopping as she opens it. "And for God's sake, clean up this room. It looks like a child threw a tantrum." She calls back before exiting.

Once she's gone, Felix wobbles his head and sticks out his tongue. "Clean up your mess." He repeats. "Fucking cow." He mutters as he turns to inspect the room and watch for more updates on the carnage.

Olivia quickly makes her way down to the main front entrance of the manor where Wellington, a tall distinguished looking man dressed in a traditional chauffeur uniform is waiting, holding the rear door open to her silver Jubilee Rolls Royce Phantom.

"Is everything okay?" Wellington asks as she's getting in, he's concerned. He's spent his entire working career with her and believes he's more of a confidant than a driver. She nods her head and smiles. "Just another incompetent fool." She remarks as she takes her seat. He quickly closes the door, jumps into the driver's seat and they speed away.

As they drive, Wellington glances in the rear view mirror observing the celebratory expression on Olivia's face. "Ma'am?" he asks.

"Mark my words Wellington. This day…September eleventh, two thousand and one, is going to be the dawn of a new era."

CHAPTER ONE

"What the fuck is going on?" Frank wonders unaware that he's four stories down in a secure bunker, as he watches Bertram walk over to Oin and Stogie bound to chairs and cuts their binds, pushing his black wire rimmed glasses back up on his nose as he uprights.

Zach looks at Frank. "I haven't a clue." He says, reading Frank's mind.

Bertram, a slim adult version of Harry Potter and still dressed in a three piece tweed suit and bowtie, frees Zach before ridding Frank of his bonds. Frank elects to remain seated as the other three get out of their chairs and he watches the odd-ball group consisting of Willow, Reggie, Scott and his supposed brethren of the Tsiatko clan in front of him, as they eye him. Frank's gaze targets Garth Scott, the strangest looking one of the bunch with his Cossack cut hair, Amish style beard, his tall lean frame still adorned in a two piece grey suit and dress shirt now clearly spattered in blood. The very one who, just a few minutes ago was threatening to fry him with a commercial grade battery charger, now is staring back at him with a slight smirk on his face.

Oin and Stogie move over to where Willow stands. "That went pretty smooth." Oin says grinning as Gaylord, Frank's Tsiatko bodyguard, gently pats him on the shoulder.

"Like clockwork." Stogie adds as he pulls out a cigar and starts chomping down on it. Willow just nods and smiles, glancing at Frank.

Zach walks behind his chair and leans on its backrest, not sure what to make of it all or what to do; he's not looking impressed about matters.

Frank bows his nodding head. It's beginning to sink in that he was a pawn, just a piece in the game that this outfit used to reach a means to an end and he doesn't like it. He's feeling the fool, especially in front of all these people he knows nothing about. He pushes himself out of the chair, stretching his neck and takes a position similar to Zach's behind his own chair. The two of them watch and wait in silence.

Willow approaches Frank. She can see he's hurt. "Frank, I'm sorry but it's not about you. It's about the world." She says sincerely.

A single tear involuntarily runs down his cheek. He feels betrayed, used, embarrassed and she gently wipes it away. He's not feeling much like a man at the moment and looks down to the grey concrete floor. Willow places her hand on his head and gives it a soft stroke.

Zach turns to face the wall, crossing his arms as he leans lightly back on the chair. His feelings are similar as he now knows he was used as well. At this moment, he's not feeling very jubilant about being free but no one comes to comfort him.

Frank takes a couple big breaths. He knows he has to push past his feelings and suck it up. He looks up. "Why the big charade?" He asks.

Willow looks back at the group and over at the dead bodies piled to the side. "Let's go someplace more hospitable to talk." She says. Reggie leads the way. They are a sight, several humans followed by the Tsiatko as they proceed down the wing of the posh underground bunker and move into the kitchen where Brother instructs most of the Tsiatko to remain. The rest of the group continues to the living area.

"Quite the digs." Frank says sarcastically as he looks across at the rec room before entering the living area.

"Get use to them, this'll be your new home for awhile." Reggie says.

Frank stops. "What do you mean?"

"We'll get to that." Willow interjects. "Sit…please."

Frank gazes at the imitation skylights, the forged exterior views and the pure over the top luxury before sitting down on one of the several large, high end couches in the room. The rest take various spots with Zach choosing one that places the greatest distance between him and Reggie and it doesn't go unnoticed. Brother and Gaylord remain standing near the entranceway. "Well," Frank says as he looks around the room before studying Willow. "Put it all together for me because…I don't have a clue. I mean, what're you doing working with the

Committee and how did you con him?" Indicating Brother, his Tsiatko brethren. "Or is this part of the same trap you laid for me way back at Rainier? Christ." Frank gets up, shaking his head, rubbing his face again. "There's no way you could have pulled this off without Zach's help." He faces them all, his arms out stretched. "Am I the only one not in on this?"

"Frank, I had nothing," Zach begins.

Willow abruptly turns to Zach, pointing a finger at him. "Shut up!" She demands before returning her attention to Frank. "They're not the Committee, they're Handlers."

Zach jumps up. "Bullshit to that! Jesus, I worked for them. I know who the Committee is and who's not. What kind of crap is this?"

Willow rises and faces Zach. "Rein it in! This explanation is for Frank, not you. Your fate is still up in the air." She warns.

Zach receives cold stares from Oin, Stogie and Bertram and a threatening look from Scott while Reggie's face is emotionless. Brother and Gaylord do not give him the time of day so he reluctantly sits back down.

Willow turns to Frank. "They're a team just like us. We didn't know they were here until recently. Like us, they weren't prepared to give up. Their methods," Willow says nodding to Reggie before looking back at Frank, "Are more…aggressive and they chose to go in a different direction than us by infiltrating the Committee itself. Zach's actions were all his own…that is, until we sent him back to Reggie." Willow says smiling.

"And as for Willow's team, we didn't know they were here either until Willow contacted me. Well, sort of didn't know." Reggie says smirking. "I didn't recognize any of them but when I used facial software on an ATM picture of Oin and got hits going back a few centuries, I suspected. Willow got a hold of me shortly after. She had a plan in place but after some discussions, we made some modifications and here we are." Reggie states.

Frank sits. "Nothing's that simple. How'd you find out about the other team?" He asks Willow.

"At the Sherriff's office when they came to get Zach. Unlike Oin, Scott has a way of standing out, someone you would remember." She laughs.

Frank sees these two teams of Handlers are right at home with each other. Why shouldn't they be?

Willow continues. "The guys wouldn't have recognized him without binoculars; he was too far away and moving too fast. I needed to be sure so I reached out to Reggie. It's a simple process to contact another Handler if you need to."

Frank was watching all their faces as Willow spoke, their story has credence and he could see it in their eyes that she was speaking the truth. Frank's feeling a little less defensive, foolish and hurt. These Handlers have thousands of years of experience and frustrations invested in this process while he's been playing it by ear. He may have been created in earlier times during previous occupations but all memories of those died with his each of his passings, with each of the failures. "And the Tsiatko?" Frank asks.

Willow walks to Brother. "The night I had Oin be there for you with the van and after you left for Seattle, I went searching in the cavern for the Tsiatko. I announced who I was and they came. It didn't take much to convince him I was a Handler. Once they accepted that fact, they were more concerned as to what I could do to them as opposed to what they could do to me." Willow says, placing her hand on Brother's arm to demonstrate as much respect as she can as she speaks of their arrangement. "We talked about what we both wanted for this planet and our passion for its continued existence. We negotiated terms, part of which was allowing you and Zach to escape. We also made a pact to work in harmony against the Committee and to do what was required to preserve this place for all life. So with the Tsiatko's help, we've made it this far."

"Great, everyone is working hand in hand, Kumbaya and all that. But for what? What's the end game? I still don't understand why the pretense and the masquerade…why slaughter everyone?" Frank asks.

It's Reggie's turn to speak up and she stands to do so. "Why? It's because the Committee was watching Belette like a hawk. They're watching everyone especially after Zach went AWOL. Zach can even testify to that." She says nodding in his direction. "Not that I'm going to let him give his two cents worth right now." She warns. "And I'm sure they have me under a microscope as well. We had no idea as to the extent of their surveillance, satellite, bugs, video…spies, so we had to make everything, every detail, action, discussion seem legit. The only place that's secure is in here, deep in the confines of this bunker." Reggie leans back on one leg crossing her arms. "You call it slaughter; I call it starting with the required clean slate."

Frank turns back to Willow. "And you're good with this?" Before she can answer, he looks around. "You're all okay with this?" He asks.

"Absolutely." Willow says as the others simply nod. "A big part of this is to protect you. Our cover story is that we repelled an attack, one led by you. That we took out insurgents who had infiltrated Felix's security teams and with your declared death in this battle, we've eliminated Frank Smirnov, the dreaded hybrid, the one thing the Committee feared most…all thanks to Zach's covert scheme of pretending to befriend an old school mate. With no witnesses to dispute Reggie's version of events, it'll further elevate her status and let her continue to move up the ranks of the Committee while giving you someplace safe and secure to live. We'll even take DNA samples from all those who have died, including yours to prove our side of events."

"And you think this will help make a difference?" Frank asks disparagingly.

Willow moves toward Frank. "You know why we have failed for so long, so many times? I had to look down deep for the answers, I had an epiphany and I didn't like what I realized but ultimately it was the only logical answer…it's because of men. Always trying to run the show, more worried about who had the bigger dick, rather than getting the job done right the first fucking time. Excuse my French but I'm," She looks at Reggie. "WE"RE sick and tired of it. We love the men on our teams." She says as she scans their faces. "But even they know we're right. These damn occupations, the playbook for these…experiments, written by men, directed by men and every damn one a complete failure."

"As I move up," Reggie adds to the discussion. "I'm taking Willow and her team with me. We're going to take down the Committee from the inside and we Handlers, led by women are taking over the show."

"And there are more of us, other Handlers floating around out there in space because they don't know what to do with themselves, with a wait and see attitude about what transpires here. We're bringing them all back." Willow says. "There WILL be fruit from our labors."

Frank knows she could be one hundred percent right but whether it's men or women, Handler or human, to him it sounds like it could easily become a dictatorship. "Then what, men become second rate citizens?" Frank asks.

Willow looks like she's going to explode. "Second rate?!" She pokes her finger hard into Frank's chest. "My point exactly! When women are in that role, no problem. We want to put men in it, now its second rate?!" I thought you were better than that?!" She almost shouts.

"That's not what I meant." Frank says trying to back pedal. Willow only stares him down. There's a side of her that has emerged that Frank didn't see coming. His manhood is taking a hit again and he's not sure how good he'll be at swallowing his pride, taking orders, not being in control. If he does, will he ever be able to reclaim it? Frank changes the topic slightly, hopefully to his benefit. "You said this is going to be my home. It sounds like it's could end up being more like a prison. What am I suppose to be doing here?" He asks.

Willow takes a deep breath, trying to calm herself, second guessing her outburst and turns to Brother who gives instructions in his native tongue to Gaylord. He leaves and they all wait in uncomfortable silence for several moments until his return. He's carrying a worn, military green canvas satchel which he hands to Willow. She sets it down on a coffee table and gently removes a round object heavily wrapped with a tattered yellowed cloth which she places in a large glass platter in the centre the table and gently uncovers it, revealing the Orb. "You're going to start earning your keep, voluntarily of course." She announces.

Frank isn't surprised. "And Zach, what's to become of him?" Frank asks wondering and hoping he'll be of some value to Frank even though the warning from Mr. H still haunts him. "Trust no one."

"Leave him to me." Reggie interjects. "Don't worry Frank; he'll be kept alive, earning his keep as well…maybe not as voluntarily as you." She states.

Zach makes eye contact with her. He's not sure whether he should be excited about that news. He looks over at Frank who gives him a slight nod. They both know they're going to have to make an allegiance, a serious one this time, as this is scenario neither of them planned or want and this is further confirmed by Frank's eyes and expression. Frank's look clearly communicates to Zach that he's not about to take a backseat on this ride and he wonders if anyone else can read this as well. He quickly scans the room but none of the Handlers, Willow, Reggie, Oin, Stogie, Bertram or Scott, are paying them any heed. They all have momentarily lost interest in the two of them and are now engrossed in conversations about their recent conquest. He glances back to Frank whose gaze is now locked in with Brother. If Zach didn't know better he'd think they were communicating telepathically. A moment later Frank smiles as Brother leans over to Gaylord, whispers in his ear and they head for the doorway. Zach gets up and attempts to follow but by the time he reaches the hallway, they've vanished…Brother, Gaylord, all of the Tsiatko. Zach turns back to the room, looking to Frank, wondering what the hell just happened but Frank is ignoring him. It takes a minute for the Handlers to realize the Tsiatko's departure.

"Where are Gaylord and Brother?" Oin asks as he checks the room then heads for the hallway. "They're gone. All of them." He states as he re-enters.

"Don't worry." Willow says. "We'll let them be, leave them to their wilderness playground. They've played their part. We're in control now." If Willow only knew as to who, or what, was really in control.

Reggie speaks up now. "It's time fto put our celebration on hold. We need to get to work. We have a lot of obstacles ahead of us yet and, a lot of clean up. Scott, you and Bertram okay with the body detail?" She asks.

"We're fine with that." Scott says, not waiting for Bertram to agree.

"Don't forget to get a DNA sample from each body and match it with their I.D." Willow interjects. "We may have to do some proving with the Committee. Oin and Stogie, you two good with giving them a hand?"

"No problem." Stogie mutters out between chews of his cigar. "Oin said he wanted to be part of the action, this is the down side." He adds laughing as he gives Oin a solid slap on the shoulder. "C'mon my man, time to learn how to dispose of bodies."

"This sucks." Oin remarks.

Bertram shakes his head remembering not only the bloody mess in the storage room but the body parts strewn about in the main entranceway of the bunker… everywhere actually, the handy work of the Tsiatko. "Seriously?" He asks.

"Hey, why do you think wheel barrows and bleach were invented?" Scott chuckles. "But your right, this isn't going to be fun but we need to get at it before the stench rolls in."

"And me?" Zach asks.

"You're going with them my little runaway." Willow says with a gleam in her eyes. "You're far from being trusted but you have so much to contribute. Why else do you think you're still around?" She asks. "So let's put you to good use in the meantime…unless you would prefer the alternative?"

"I'm not sure I want an answer to that." Zach replies with a slight shake of his head as he joins the others.

"Smart man," Willow says. "Smart man."

"Reggie and I are heading to the main house." Willow calls as the clean-up crew moves out leaving only Frank in the room with them. "Frank," Willow says turning her attention to him "Do we have to worry about leaving you here on your own?"

Frank hesitates before answering. "No…you don't. It's not like this is something I can walk away from and I'm not referring to your suggestion of me being confined here in any way. I mean, I know I'm here to make a difference and I will." He says letting them interpret that any way they want.

Willow walks to him and gently grabs him by the hand sending a spark of electricity through him once more as he tries not to let his attraction to her show. "Frank, sorry for my little tantrum and I know this has been tough for you. All these revelations in such a short time and then this…display, these theatrics but we had no choice. It's about salvation, reclamation and redemption for this world. I hope you understand that?" She says.

Frank watches as the words escape past her sensual lips and he searches her beautiful alluring eyes for signs of the truth. He finds no answers and chooses to whisper his answer in her ear. "I do." He says as he slowly steps back letting go. "Can I not even trust her?" He asks himself…asks Mr. H. She smiles, turns and the two Handler leaders leave. Frank breathes a sigh of relief. He's finally alone, just him and the Orb, and he's going to put the time to good use.

CHAPTER TWO

Reggie leads Willow back to the main house. As they stroll Willow can't help but be impressed by the grounds, they are so much more beautiful in person than the images from Google Earth. Not beautiful in the way of flowers and adornments but in design with a combination of several terraces comprised of lush green lawns, red brick pathways, immense fountains, manicured hedges and trees of every shape and genus. They seem so meticulously kept but at the same time appear as if they're very low maintenance. This would make sense especially if they wanted to keep the personnel on site to a minimum. They approach the matching Arcola Red interlocking stone lane that originates from the highway where the security gates and guard house are located and stroll along it as it mutates into a wide circular driveway, with an elaborate twenty foot cream white cast stone fountain in its centre, and continue past as the lane morphs into a walkway then steps leading to the manor's main entrance. For Willow, this house…manor… mansion, whatever term is used to describe this monstrosity of waste, she has to admit, it's spectacular looking especially with the endless forests rolling along the picturesque snow capped mountains set in its background. The mansion is a traditional design three story brick with a center main complex and wings extending out from either side. White columns tower from the ground to the matching covered entranceway and she notices all the windows throughout reach from floor to ceiling on every level, their rectangular multi-pane frames painted a glistening white with matching security grates covering each one.

"I know," Reggie says. "A bit lavish and over the top. It has a spa, a natatorium, a library, and even a leather-walled billiard room. Its old school, designed by men living that chauvinistic life style but you'll definitely find it comfortable."

"Find it comfortable?" Willow responds. "I hope so. This is crazy." They enter into a polished Cappuccino marbled floor rotunda and climb the expansive circular dark mahogany staircase to the second floor. As they reach the second level, twenty-two feet up, Willow stops to look down. "I feel guilty just being in here. How do they justify this, while so many suffer?" She says shaking her head as she turns to Reggie.

Reggie doesn't stop and remains mute as they walk. "Come on." She finally says. "Let me show you where we'll mainly be working out of. You better get use to this if you want to blend in with the Committee. If you can't at least feint enjoying this opulent lifestyle, you're not going to last." Reggie warns. They move down the hallway and enter Reggie's office. Willow stops at the doorway to check out the room, a frown on her face as she inspects the interior. "Is something wrong?" Reggie asks.

"Not the décor I envisioned you'd have." Willow answers, grimacing.

Reggie laughs. "It's from my predecessor. I was hoping my interior designer was going to begin soon but now with everything moving forward, I imagine I'm going to have to suffer with it for awhile yet."

"Whew, thank God for that, I know I have to get use to things but this…no way." Willow giggles.

Reggie remains straight faced. "Let's sit a minute." She says as she takes a seat in the Regency Lazy Chair and Willow chooses the Balmoral tufted leather couch. "I just want to clear the air and make sure there are no misunderstandings."

"About what?" Willow asks.

"Us." Reggie says. "I know we are on my home turf here but I need you to know that I consider us equals on this endeavor. I'm not your boss, you're not mine and we share the leadership equally. We make all the decisions together, when we can. I realize some have to be made on the fly and we can't always consult each other but I want you to understand that I trust you explicitly."

Willow sits back. "Wow, I've been so engrossed in things that this potential issue never crossed my mind. You're right in bringing it up and I feel the same way."

"Good," Reggie replies. "For appearance purposes for the Committee you'll be my newly appointed second in command, roles do have to be played. Oh, I hope you don't mind taking my old office and bedroom?"

"Not at all, what about the backgrounds for us we talked about? I'd be surprised if the Committee just takes your word. No offence but I'm sure they'll do their due diligence."

"Already done," Reggie says. "I have a jacket prepared on each of you that is impeccable and will withstand any scrutiny. I have copies on my desk for the three of you to familiarize yourselves with. I already had a video conference scheduled with the Committee members for tomorrow, so I'll be forwarding them with my report on today's events ASAP, along with my endorsement on your team and we'll see where it goes from there."

"I have to ask, did they accept you, a woman, with open arms to this AR position? From what you've told me, this appears to be more of a boy's club and has been for a long time." Willow says.

"They have and so far, no repercussions but I've been playing it like a hard ass. From my end, I have no idea if there are any women currently on the Committee board or whether that would make a difference as far as my acceptance, they keep their identities quite secretive. My saving grace is that the head of the Committee for decades; actually was a woman, named Olivia Kinsey. She's gone now but from what little I was able to find, she was tough as nails but you wouldn't know it looking at her. She was a smaller woman, refined, elegant, supposedly came from old money but she was one no one dared cross. From what I've heard, she's buried more than a few bodies…casualties of those that didn't take her seriously." Reggie answers.

"Okay, what's next then?" Willow replies.

"First," As Reggie hands her a flash drive, "This is everything I have on the Committee, current and the past. Study it as best you can, the more you know the better. There's a laptop in my old office."

"Perfect." Willow replies tucking it in her jeans pocket.

"Our first priority is security. While the guys are cleaning up, we'll start sweeping for bugs and cameras. It's going to take time but we need to know for sure we can quit the theatrics. Once we have that done, I have an idea on how to minimize our own defense needs and reduce potential Committee spies. I know the Committee will be suspicious after they review my report but I think I've proven my worth." Reggie says.

"And how receptive are they going to be about Zach's return?" Willow asks.

"I'll tell them the plan that kicked this off to falsely aide Frank was Zach's and approved by Felix, a decision he didn't share with the Committee for fear of the repercussions if Zach failed or double crossed him." Reggie says tapping her finger nail on the arm of her chair.

"I know there's some history between you two but I have to ask, is Zach worth the risk?" Willow says. "Does he really have anything of value?"

Reggie's tapping stops. "I'm not sure." She admits with a frown. "Enough with him, let's get on with things before I realize how tired I actually am." It's late in the night before Reggie and Willow finish their task. They do locate a few listening devices, de-activate them but there's no way to determine if they're old or new, placed on orders from Felix or the Committee's. It's going to be a wait and see game. As they return to Reggie's office, they're met by the rest of the crew who have just wrapped up their grim task.

"How'd it go?" Willow asks.

"Actually better than planned, even Zach pulled his weight out there." Scott says. "Things went especially well…once we found a commercial wood chipper under a tarp in the bunker."

"Efficient but gross." Oin adds. The clean-up crew look at Bertram, they're all smiling, even Zach. Bertram, with his Harry Potter looks is not. He's a little pasty and is shaking his head, one hand to his mouth and the other up, indicating a no response to Scott's and Oin's remarks.

"I put the DNA samples in the bar fridge in your office, all labeled and ready." Scott says.

"Did you get one from Frank?" Reggie asks.

"Yea," Stogie says. "But he was being bit of a dick and hesitant to give it up, concerned that if you gave it to the Committee to prove his death that they could use it somehow."

"I'll talk to him about it." Willow says.

"Look, you all must be beat, why don't we call it a night. I have a couple calls to make and then I'm done too." Reggie says. "Oh, I hate to ask but we need someone to man the guard house tonight until we get that sorted out, any volunteers?"

"I got it," Bertram states. "After that experience I'm not going to be able to sleep anyways."

"Well Zach," Reggie says, "You get the same bedroom you had last night. Are you with us or do we have to lock you in?" The Handlers wait for his response.

Zach combs back his long dark hair with his fingers before crossing his arms across his chest. "Hmm…let me think. Frank is here and the Tsiatko are gone, not that they really liked me that much anyways, I have no teams left that I could possibly source some help from and if I run you'll have every resource the Committee has hunting me down." Zach locks his hands behind his back and nonchalantly walks up to Reggie who does not step back with his approach. He leans in, his lips almost brushing the lobe of her ear. "And now, there's just something so intriguing about being in the company of such an older woman that…I couldn't even consider walking away." He whispers and steps back before she can react. "Based on these facts, I volunteer my services." He announces loud and clear to the rest of the Handlers and before a now slightly blushing Reggie. "Good night all." He says as he walks past her toward his bedroom. Tonight, he'll need to find a way to get to Frank.

Reggie immediately walks the opposite direction to her office leaving the rest of the Handlers where they stand. "I have calls to make." She says attempting to conceal her blushing face. She's conflicted about Zach but smiles as she walks, his hushed words still resonating in her ear.

Willow bites her lip and remains silent. She's having difficulty with having Zach here as she's sure Oin and Stogie are too, but they all agreed to the plan. What value he has in their battle against the Committee will still have to be proved. As the rest of the Handlers make their way past her to their rooms, she gently grabs Oin by the arm. "Keep an eye on Zach." She whispers and he waves his acknowledgement as he moves on.

Richard Montgomery parks his frame on a stool at the long wooden counter and nurses a frothing mug of brew in yet another local hang out. Where this place is he's not sure as he's been randomly driving his rental from town to town the last couple of days, ever since he left Rainier, still trying to grasp what's happened. He pulls the military green cap off his sparse and graying crew cut hair and inspects the reflection of the forty-five year old guy looking back at him in the mirror behind the bar. He has a plump face and portly build but it wasn't always that way, he's five ten and two hundred pounds of soft muscle, as he likes to describe it. The flab is from too much time seated behind a console as an UAV pilot followed by years confined in mobile units as head of a drone division. In a blink of an eye, he's gone from being a highly regarded leader of a covert drone team to unemployment and has laid witness to events and…things that he was not meant to see, understand or believe. The saving grace is that he's sitting on a pile of cash, severance pay from Reggie Byrnes, a ruthless bitch of a woman that frightens the hell out of him and hopes to never cross paths with again. His cell goes off and as much as he wants to ignore it, he pulls it out from the side pocket of his kaki green jacket…as he does so he wonders why he's still wearing this military shit. He has to face reality and get some civvies. He looks at the screen wondering who could be calling and recognizes the number. "No fucking way." He says to no one other than himself and disconnects the call. Moments later it rings again. "Shit!" He's scared to answer it but more so if he doesn't. He takes a deep breath. "Montgomery here." He says hesitantly.

On the other end of the call, Reggie is laughing. "I was wondering how many times I'd have to call before you answered." She states as she leans back in her office chair and props her feet, still donning designer high heels, up on the desk.

"Ms. Byrnes…I'm surprised to hear from you." He says.

"I bet you are."

"Uh…what can I do for you?"

"Why, I'm so glad you asked considering all the money I've paid you. It shows your appreciation and willingness to repay me any way you can." Reggie says smiling wishing she could see his facial expression.

"Ms. Byrnes…ma'am, I owe you but to be honest…what you're into, is…way beyond me." He says timidly.

"Don't worry. What I have is a simple security detail, nothing more, just you and your pilots operating drones on an estate."

"Listen, I appreciate the offer but I have to pass." Montgomery says nervously. He guzzles down his beer and waves to the bartender for another glass of liquid courage.

Reggie swings her feet down to the floor. "I wasn't making a request. I LET you and your team walk away from the last job, remember that or would you have preferred ending up facing a fate similar to your comrades in that cavern!" She barks out. Her bad ass persona has taken over.

"Fuck!" The word involuntarily slips from Montgomery's mouth. "Sorry ma'am…not what I meant to say." As he grabs a napkin off the bar to wipe the sweat now streaming down his furrowed brow.

There's silence at the other end.

"Ma'am?"

"Yes Montgomery?" Reggie answers.

"Sorry, thought maybe you hung up on me."

"Neither of us would want that would we?" She says.

"No ma'am." Montgomery says meekly.

"I'll send you the directions. Locate your team and I'm giving you twenty-four hours to get here. Am I understood?"

"Yes ma'am."

"See you soon and travel safe." Reggie says cheerfully and ends the call.

Montgomery checks his watch and then his pants. For a moment there he thought he wet himself.

CHAPTER THREE

As much as syncing with the Orb should feel new to Frank, it doesn't and it's nothing like his first experience in the cavern when the Tsiatko and Zach introduced it to him. Then, it felt foreign, now, it's as if it's welcoming him…when he melds with it, he's enveloped in a cocoon and all the Orb contains, its knowledge…the past, the present and the future with all its possibilities is absorbed and retained. The very fabric he's engulfed in is like a favorite song but he can't hear it, it's as if every note from all the various instruments that contribute to its creation is penetrating, resonating and flowing through his body and deposited within him…each session with the Orb is like a new melody, a new experience, a new learning. Each time it strengthens him, not physically but internally, deep within…he's enhanced him with the wisdom of the ages, with the power of time. The syncing advances quicker than he could have imagined but it's tiring him out and he emerges from its fold aware now, he's lost all track of time once again. He knows he's been at it for days but when he checks his phone, he's only been at it for hours. What the fuck but before he can make sense of it, the pangs of not eating and drinking for whatever length of time its been, are hitting him hard. He's feeling weak because of the lack of nutrition. He disconnects from the blue sphere before him and finds himself disorientated. He's having trouble…he can't comprehend how he's feeling, something he's never felt before, the Orb is…throwing him out of kilter. It's as if he's have trouble distinguishing reality from real if that makes any sense. It barely does to him…but it does.

"This thing is fucking me up." He murmurs as he heads for the kitchen still unsure of how much time has passed, days or hours.

"Look at you, you're wasting away. Sit, sit you have to eat. I have some fresh homemade soup with the dumplings you like so much." Dasha says to him as she stirs the pot of thick broth on the modern stainless steel commercial stove in front of her. Frank hesitates entering further but he can smell the inviting aroma of the soup and his stomach growls in response. Dasha is a short stout woman with dark hair and is wearing wire rim glasses. She's dressed in a tea dress covered with a white apron and she has flat black shoes on her feet. Dasha is his great aunt but he calls…called her grandma, she's the one that raised him. Trouble is… she's been dead for untold years now. "What's the matter with you?" She asks as she fills a bowl and places it on the long granite topped island. "Don't just stand there looking at me, sit and eat before it gets cold." She orders wiping her hands on her apron.

"Jesus Christ." Franks says spinning around in a single step and motors back to the living area he came from. He stops and presses his fingers to his forehead and takes a deep breath. "Fuck!" He exclaims.

"What have I said to you about swearing?" Dasha calls out from the kitchen.

Frank back pedals a couple steps and arches his back so he can peek back into the kitchen. Dasha is cutting a loaf of fresh bread and is stacking it on a platter on the island beside a small plate of butter. The smell of the hot loaf fills the room.

"What are you doing?" Dasha asks with a puzzled look on her face.

Frank erects himself and moves quickly back into the living area again. "Okay…just breath, just breath." He says out loud to himself shaking his head violently to try and clear his mind. There's no one there, remember that, no one is there." He turns and struts confidently back into the kitchen.

Frank stops in his tracks as he enters. Ivan is now sitting on the opposite side of the island on one of the many black and chrome barstools. His beard is still full and gray and he's dressed in his usual blue denim bib coveralls and white shirt. The grey wool fedora that is usually placed on his bald head is sitting to the side and he's sipping a cup of instant coffee, Frank can tell by its unmistakable smell and he suddenly yearns for its distinct taste. Ivan, his great uncle and surrogate grandpa, passed a long time ago too, the same time as Dasha almost.

"Ivan, talk to the boy. Help him make some sense of it all." Dasha insists.

"Frank, we're not here in life for us…we're here for everyone else." His grandpa says, hitting him with more words of wisdom. Most of his grandpa's sayings, which Frank had heard so often, are embedded in his brain. This…is a new one.

Frank doesn't move or speak as he fears interacting with these apparitions will only drag him into this perceived state of delirium even further.

"Frank? Frank? Frank?! What's the matter with you?" Ivan says as he gets up and walks toward him. "Frank? Frank!" Ivan almost shouts as he grabs Frank by the shoulder and gives him a good shake.

"Frank! Frank!" Stogie shouts. "What the hell is the matter with you?" He asks as he shakes Frank some more.

"Shit!" Frank exclaims, his mouth is agape and his eyes wide and black as he jolts back to…reality?

"Christ Frank, where were you man? It's like you were looking right through me?" Stogie asks.

Frank remains stationary; his eyes return to normal as he checks the room for Dasha and Ivan, while the clean-up crew gawks at him. He's trying to find any evidence that his manifestations are, were…real but there's nothing, no scent of instant coffee, no pot of fresh soup on the stove, no aroma of fresh baked bread or a crumb as evidence of its existence on the island.

"Frank, you okay?" Zach asks concerned.

Frank says nothing only shifts his eyes back and forth at everyone now present in the room with him, still unsure whether to interact in any way, trying to determine what realm of reality he's in.

"Look Frank, we need a DNA sample from you, bosses' orders. They need it for the Committee." Scott says. Frank gives no response, just remains motionless so Scott takes advantage of his open mouth and takes a swab. "Okay, we're good then. See ya Frank." He says giving a "Is he a nut case?" look and steps away. The rest of the crew hesitantly follows Scott as he leaves.

Frank, still uneasy of what is unfolding, finally turns and shouts out his first coherent thought "Hey, make sure the Committee can't screw around with that sample!"

"We hear you Frank, we hear you." Stogie says.

Zach is walking backwards, trying to analyze Frank's weird behavior as he exits. Something is fucked up.

Frank watches them depart. His heart is racing, he feels like he's out of control and he doesn't like it. He closes his eyes. "Breath…relax, just be calm. Another side effect from the Orb, nothing more." He tells himself. He inhales deeply, holds it for a moment and exhales all the way out. He does this a few more times before opening his eyes. "All is good, all is good." He whispers. He turns and…slams into the hairy chest of Gaylord. Frank leaps back. "Jesus fucking Christ!!" He yells, bouncing in place before bending over and placing his hands on his knees to breathe. "Holy Fuck!" He says as he tries to catch his breath, his heart pounding. "That's it…I'm going to fuckin die now."

"Did I damage you brother?" Gaylord asks sincerely with his deep, rumbling voice.

Frank looks up from his keeled over position. "No, you didn't hurt me! You scared the living shit out of me! Why would you sneak up on me that way and… what the hell are you doing here?!"

"You appeared to be deep in thought and I did not want to interrupt." Gaylord replies. "And, I am here to protect you. Brother believes you may need it now more than ever." There's an unsettled look on Gaylord's face.

Frank stands and places a hand on Gaylord's arm. "I'm sorry. I'm glad you're here, really…just please, announce yourself somehow first. My heart can't take much more." He says and chuckles, shaking his head at his own foolishness. "Are you hungry? I'm about to eat. I'm starving, so much so my mind is playing tricks on me."

'I will eat." Gaylord answers, grinning.

They both have their fill of eat and drink and do it in comfortable silence. Frank finds himself enjoying the quiet company and is entertained by the delicate manner Gaylord dines. "Well Gaylord," Frank says as he stands and stretches. "I'm beat. I'm just going to crash on a couch in there," Nodding in the direction of the living area. "Okay?"

"I do not understand crash on crouch."

"Not crouch, couch. The big pieces of furniture we sit on in there, and crash is a way of saying sleep or rest. So I am going to go sleep on one of the furniture in that room." Frank says pointing. "You can sleep anywhere you like, just make yourself at home. Understand now?"

"I do. I will…crash in there as well."

"Whatever tickles your fancy," Frank replies

"I do not understand." Gaylord says.

Frank raises both his hands in the air. "Never mind, I give up, I am too tired for this." He heads for the living room, switching off the lights as he enters and takes a seat on the nearest sofa. Gaylord strolls past but Frank pays him no mind, he's staring intensely at the blue light of the Orb. He's a bit unnerved by what he's experiencing and that's not like him. It's as if he's moving back and forth through time but he's knows that's can't be happening as it's all transpiring here within this bunker…he thinks. He's sure it's just a side effect from the Orb…or could it be something more, something in the contents of the Orb that hasn't revealed itself…shit, so much for the self-confidence in the ease of syncing with this damn thing. He looks back and sees Gaylord stretched out on the biggest couch in the room, his feet dangling off the end. Frank's glad he's here. He was concerned about leaving the Orb unattended while he slept, not that he's expecting anyone to come in and steal it, well, Zach is still around so yea, that is a possibility yet. To be on the safe side he gets up, wraps the Orb with the covering Willow had on it and stuffs it in between the cushions on the end of his sofa. Not that it's the most secure spot but he wants it near him. The room is darker now without the bright hue of the sphere so Frank plops face down on the seat cushions and quickly falls into a deep sleep but it doesn't last. He finds himself tossing and turning, a million involuntary thoughts and memories racing through his head. He decides a hot shower should relax him. This done, he heads back to the kitchen for a glass of juice before bed and discovers Ivan seated at the island reading a newspaper, The Bluff County News, published in Lanesboro, Minnesota.

He turns to Frank. "I don't know why I read this thing. These so-called college graduated politicians make me shake my head. You know education doesn't always mean a degree…and intelligence doesn't always mean common sense." Another of his sayings, one Frank has heard many times.

Frank peeks into the living area and sees that Gaylord seems oblivious to Ivan's presence. He ignores his specter visitor, opens the large commercial fridge, the door now blocking Ivan from his sight and he takes his time having a swig from the Delmonte juice container so his phantom has time to disappear. Jug in hand he gradually closes the door hoping not to come face to face with Ivan.

"Hey Frank." Zach says, standing there instead.

"Shit!" Frank says startled as the flask of juice hits the floor spilling orange liquid everywhere and Frank jumps back attempting to dodge the fluid.

"Sorry Frank, I didn't mean to surprise you like that." Zach says.

"Christ sakes!" Frank yells as he peers around Zach to see if Ivan is still sitting there but he's gone. "What the fuck is this, a conspiracy to have me drop dead in my tracks?!"

Zach takes a couple steps back to avoid the moving flow of liquid. "Jesus Frank, what's with you? Why so edgy?" Zach asks. "After the way you acted earlier, I just wanted to check up on you. You were beyond strange, the way you were behaving."

Frank puts up an open hand, silently acknowledging to Zach everything's okay. "Just…agitated, I was working with the Orb and it took a toll, that's all, something I haven't experienced before."

"So, uh…where is the Orb? I didn't see it when I walked through." Zach says with a flash of that familiar fox in the hen house look.

"Zach, I have it stashed but if you ever so much as go near it, I'll have Gaylord break you in two. Got it?" Frank warns.

"Gaylord?" Zach asks.

"Yea, Gaylord." Frank replies indicating behind Zach.

Zach looks back to see Gaylord standing there so he turns to him. "Hey Big Guy, how's it hanging?"

Gaylord looks to Frank for direction. "I do not understand." He says.

Zach laughs. "You will one day, you will," And proceeds past him into the living room.

"Keep an eye on him." Frank instructs Gaylord. "You understand THAT don't you?"

"Yes." Gaylord confirms.

"Okay, I gotta clean up this mess." Frank replies. A hand clamps down on Frank's shoulder from behind. Frank whirls around, his eyes black and his lethal strike stops a fraction of an inch from Oin's nose. "Oin, I could have killed you!" Frank exclaims dropping his hand. "Where did you get the bright idea of coming up on me like that?"

Oin, mop in hand, is a bit shaken by Frank's eyes and the nearly deadly blow. "Who snuck? I walked by in plain sight on the other side of the island while you were talking to Zach." Oin says defending himself.

Frank places both his hands on his head. "Arrrgh." Before dropping them to his side and taking a deep breath. His eyes are now clear as he looks at Oin. "Fine… please explain why YOU are here now?"

"Willow told me to keep an eye on Zach and so, I followed him here but I'm no spy or rat. I'd rather just hang with you guys and pretend to be keeping tabs on Zach plus…I prefer your company to theirs." Referring the other Handlers. "When I saw you drop the juice I thought I'd grab a mop and clean it up for you." Oin says.

Frank sighs heavily and says nothing. He returns to the living room, extracts the Orb from the cushions and takes a seat on the couch. He sits in silence staring at the Orb sitting in his lap while Zach and Gaylord curiously watch him. Minutes later, his task done, Oin enters walking past the zoned out Frank and joins Zach and Gaylord in their surveillance. Frank rises, cradling the Orb in one arm. "I'm going to one of the bedrooms to sleep, you guys do want you want just don't bug me." And he abruptly departs. As he proceeds down the hallway he looks up, "You two leave me alone as well, got it?" He demands loudly.

Oin, Zach and Gaylord are eyeing Frank as he half teeters down the long hallway. "Who do you think he was just talking too?" Oin asks.

"Reggie and Willow I imagine. That's the only thing that makes sense." Zach answers.

Oin nods. "Yea, you're probably right. You think there's any popcorn here?"

CHAPTER FOUR

As tired as Willow feels, she's wide awake with the morning sun. The events from the last few days are harboring her thoughts and not permitting her to get all the rest her body is demanding. She involuntarily groans as she sits up as her muscles remind her of the physical strain from yesterday's events, not that she overly exerted herself but she thought she was in better shape. She pushes herself upright and makes her way to the washroom refusing to look in the mirror as she showers and gets ready. She throws on a pair of Levi jeans, a unisex white T-shirt and a pair of white canvas sneakers and ties her long black hair into a ponytail before presenting herself before the six foot wide, floor to ceiling mirror in the bedroom. She turns to the side and then back front again as she examines how presentable she is, studying the image of the forty year old woman before her. She has an attractive symmetrical face with high cheek bones, a darker complexion and prefers to be make up free. She leans in close. Her big dark brown eyes still have a sparkle and she parts her full lips to reveal a bright white smile. She steps back, places her hands on her hips turning sideways again studying her shapely five foot eight athletic build as thoughts of Frank gnaw at her. "What am I doing?" She almost shouts as she drops her arms to her side. She has never been one overly concerned of her looks. "Goddamn men." She says as she heads for the door and tries to ignore anymore notions about him. She makes her way to the kitchen and enters to find Reggie already there.

Reggie's long red hair is down and a blue/white Clarice floral print button down dress covers her tall slender, long limbed physique. White leather Tabitha Simmons printed toe pumps adorn her feet elevating her height to six foot three. She's standing over the marble island reviewing notes scattered among a plate holding the remnants of a bagel, a container of cream cheese, a jar of jam, a knife and spoon sitting on a used napkin and an empty yogurt container. Reggie's piercing blue green eyes look at Willow over the brim of her coffee cup as she takes a sip of the fresh brew.

"Really?" Willow asks as she halts her advance.

Reggie lowers her cup revealing her impeccable complexion and flawless make-up application on her lightly freckled pale skin. "I know." She says surveying the island. "Bit of a mess but eating helps me think."

"God, nothing to do with that, how on earth do you look that good this early in the day?" Willow remarks.

Reggie smiles. "Practice, lots of practice. Problem is, good or bad; I'm actually enjoying it."

"I can't imagine doing that day in and day out." Willow replies as she makes her way to the coffee pot, pours a mug full and takes a seat across from Reggie. She takes an appreciative swallow of the hot rejuvenating black beverage and notices Reggie staring at her. "What?" Willow asks.

"Hate to the bearer of bad news but if you're going to play the role, you need to dress the part, full time." Reggie says. "The Committee has high expectations of all those within their inner circle and we won't know when they may want a video meet or come knocking in person."

"It's too early in the morning and I haven't had near enough coffee for this but, I knew it was inevitable, I just didn't want to hear it yet. On-line shopping, here I come." Willow announces, raising her cup in a muted cheer. "Does the same go for Oin and Stogie?"

"No, they get a free ride. Just you since you're my number two."

They'll appreciate that, especially Stogie." Willow says. Stogie with his seventy year old looks, grey hair and heavy set build is getting a little too stubborn for change…getting, always has been. Willow remembers what a chore it was getting him to actually give up the tobacco cigars he loves chomping on for the fruit and vegetable leaf ones he uses now.

"I'm a bit surprised he's still in that body. I thought he would have done a re-boot by now." Reggie says.

Willow giggles, grabs her mug with both hands and looks at it smiling before returning her attention back to Reggie, a grin still on her face. "It's like," Willow shakes her head. "It's like he's a senior citizen living on a limited income at times and wants to get the most value for his money. He figures he's got a few more miles he can put on this one before he leaves it…so I just let him be." Willow's smile fades and her expression takes a more serious tone, "Personally, I think he's just tired of the whole process, I think we all our." Reggie says nothing and they sit in silence, each of them reflecting on their own opinions and experiences with this seemingly never ending cycle of occupations. "Okay," Willows says, breaking the quiet as she turns to scan the kitchen. "The smell of bacon is driving me crazy. Were you cooking in here before I came in?"

"Not me, Garth and Stogie were. They were here when I came down. They made scrambled eggs, grilled some bacon and butter fried diced potatoes with chopped green onions for everyone. The extras are in those covered skillets on the stove."

Willow puts a hand to her chest. "Those guys are life savers. I'm starving. Where are they now?"

"Garth was going to relieve Bertram at the gate so Stogie went to walk him down before going to check on Oin and Zach. Do you think Frank has stayed put?" Reggie asks.

"I hope so. We haven't left him a lot of options. As soon as I eat, I'll take a plate down to him as well and check up on him." Willow says as she walks over and starts filling a platter for herself.

"He didn't seem too happy about the arrangement." Reggie replies.

Willow stops momentarily to look back at Reggie. "He's the one factor we have limited control over. He and the Orb are meant to be together. Where he takes things from here hopefully corresponds with our agenda."

Reggie waits until Willow is seated again. "Do you think he's sold on our game plan?" Reggie asks.

"No." Willow says without hesitation. "But I do believe we all want the same thing. What's all the paperwork for?" Referring to the documents Reggie has spread out before her.

"I have that video conference this afternoon with the Committee members, the ones specifically responsible for the North American Chapter…trying to prepare myself as best I can as I have one shot at selling all this to them."

"Do I need to be there?"

"No, just me…them and their secrecy. I don't know how they can be so paranoid. Each member is represented by a shadow image, they have blurred backgrounds to give no hint of their location and they all use voice changing software. I'm the only one that's fully exposed. Far as I know, one of them could be the guy working the gas pumps up the road."

"So you have no idea who they actually are or where they're located?" Willow asks.

"None."

"Sounds like our work is cut out for us." Willow says.

"We all knew this wasn't going to be easy." Reggie replies as if to reiterate their previous discussions.

"Nothing worthwhile ever is." Willow remarks.

Reggie's cell phone goes off. "Yes?" She answers.

"I have a couple deputies at the gate from Ashford. One is driving a Humvee he says you requested to be dropped off." Garth states. "What are you staring at?!"

"What?" Reggie replies.

"Sorry, not you, I was yelling at one of the dicks in the car." Garth says.

"Treat them nice." Reggie instructs him. "They must've been driving all night. Have them leave the Humvee at the gate and tell them to thank the Sheriff on my behalf."

"Will do." Garth says. "No, it's not a Chinese hair style, it's fucking Cossack!" She hears him yell out with his Aussie accent before she ends the call.

"What's that all about?" Willow asks.

"You know that security problem we have? Well, I recruited the mobile drone unit that was at Rainier when the Tsiatko took out the teams to cover us here. I had the Sheriff drop off their Humvee that holds the pilot's operating stations and Richard Montgomery, who heads up the team along with his three pilots, will be here later today. I'll have them take shifts monitoring the property with high tech drones. No need for any extra bodies floating around." Reggie says. "We'll put them in the guest house away from the main house so we don't have any intrusions."

"You trust them that much?" Willow asks.

"Not so much as trust as they owe me. I let them walk away from Rainier and gave them a huge payout for their silence, plus I know I scare the pants off of Montgomery so I doubt he'll cross us in any way."

"I'm good with that." Willow says smiling. "Fear's a good motivation."

With that, a disheveled Bertram comes shuffling into the kitchen. "Morning." He says as he sets his automatic on the island, walks to the stove and fills a plate. "Good night." And he shambles his way out.

With his exit, Stogie enters. "I can't find Oin or Zach anywhere." He says.

"Where'd you look?" Willow asks.

"All through the main house, checked the guest house and the grounds." He states.

"Did you check the bunker?" Willow says.

"Not yet. Thought I'd let you know first." Stogie replies.

"Okay, can you go to the front gate and bring in the Humvee that the Deputies just delivered so Garth doesn't have to leave the gate unattended. Reggie and I will check out the bunker." Willow says.

"Humvee? Never mind, I got it." Stogie says leaving.

"Zach…I should have known better." Reggie says shaking her head in disbelief as she picks up Bertram's weapon.

The two of them cautiously enter the bunker and make their way past the fleet of vehicles to the stairs by the elevator. Reggie takes the lead, gun at the ready, as they descend the four stories to the main rotunda entrance of the luxurious accommodations of this facility. Once at the bottom, Reggie removes her heels so she can move silently along the decorative ceramic flooring as they proceed down the expansive hallway. There's noise ahead, emanating from the living area directly across from the recreation room. As they approach, Reggie signals to Willow to halt as she continues to the entranceway a few feet away. With her gun raised she quickly peeks in. She looks in again, this time slowly and lowers her weapon. She turns to Willow. "You're not going to believe this." She says as she steps into the room and Willow follows. There's a movie playing on the expansive screen of the TV, Oin, Zach and Gaylord are in a deep slumber on the various couches. A couple of empty bowls are sitting on the floor with evidence of their popcorn contents littered across the carpet. Reggie looks down at the automatic she's holding and feels the fool for distrusting Zach so easily. She feels relief seeing him sleeping peacefully on the sofa but she also wants to kick his ass for making her go through the emotional turmoil she's just experienced. "Goddamn men." She mutters.

Willow breathes a sigh of relief. "I was worried there for a bit." She says.

Reggie turns to her. "No comment." She remarks through pursed lips.

"I see Gaylord is back." Willow says.

"Is that a problem?" Reggie asks.

"Not sure not that it really surprises me as he's Frank's assigned guardian. Thing is, I'm as apprehensive of them as they are of us. When I met with Brother in the cavern at Rainier, I may have exaggerated about our capabilities to get his cooperation hoping he wouldn't call my bluff. I'm still not sure if the Tsiatko helped for fear of repercussions from us or if they have an end game of their own, possibly including Frank."

"So…where is Frank and the Orb?" Reggie asks. The two of them move across the corridor to the rec room, it's empty.

"Where are the bedrooms?" Willow asks.

"Down there." Reggie says pointing to one of the wings. They check each room, one by one. There are twenty in total. As they move their way down the seemingly endless hallway with no results, a slight sense of panic rolls in. They locate Frank in the very last one. His location given away by the soft glow of the Orb tucked between the pillows of a king size bed, easily visible in the dark even with its wrapping. They creep in to verify Frank's presence and find him buried under a mound of covers sound asleep so they let him be and sneak back out, gently closing the door behind them.

Frank stirs and looks out from under the covers. He can sense someone in the room and sees a figure standing at the foot of the bed. He doesn't feel threatened as he struggles to focus his eyes in the dark to make out who it is.

"It's time for you to learn the truth, come visit us. Don't worry; we're still where you think we are." His grandpa says.

Frank bolts upright and checks the end of the bed, there's no one there… the damn visions are even invading his sleep. He turns to check the Orb, it's still where he parked it. He tosses back the covers, feels his way to the washroom of this unfamiliar space and squints as he reluctantly turns on the lights to ensure his aim. He showers, soaking in the hot water for several minutes before he slowly turns it cold to try and clear his head and reluctantly redresses in the same clothes he had on yesterday as he has nothing of his in this room. He leaves the Orb where it lay and heads for the door, he's dying for a coffee. He pauses as he grabs hold of the door knob, he's suddenly feeling disoriented once more. He's now hesitant to exit, unsure what world he'll be entering. The real one, the reality one or a combination of both again…this is getting fucked up.

CHAPTER FIVE

Reggie barely glances at the Humvee that Stogie brought up as she and Willow walk past, not giving it any mind as they re-enter the mansion, she has other matters weighing heavily on her mind. They've left Zach and Oin where they lay in the bunker, a couple less things to fret about while they're game planning. Reggie has to sell her story to the Committee before they can implement their next move so the less to interfere with her thoughts, the better. She calls Garth at the gate to scratch another matter off her list.

"Yes?" He answers.

"I'm expected a group of men to arrive sometime today, there should be four of them. The boss of the group is named Richard Montgomery." Reggie replies.

"What time?"

"Not sure. Last night I gave them twenty-four hours to get here and I'm hoping they're worried enough to get here sooner than that." Reggie says.

"For what?" Garth asks.

"Our new security detail. A drone unit. That's what the Humvee is for. It holds their operating stations. We lock everything down and strictly monitor from the air."

"And access?"

"They get none. They use the guest house only and we keep them on the grounds. We get groceries delivered weekly so they can just add what they need to our list when we order."

"What's Montgomery look like?" Garth asks.

"Weak." Reggie says, ending the conversation.

A couple of hours later Richard Montgomery is at the wheel of a dark SUV that pulls up to the security gates. He glances back at his three pilots who are napping on the rear bench seats as he throws the vehicle into park and waits. He was fortunate they had simply hung around Castle Rock, just outside Mt. St. Helens, while deciding what their next step should be. He's drag-ass tired as he's been driving for most of the night and rests his head on the wheel. He's brought back to life by a knock on the window and is startled by the towering sight of Garth Scott peering at him with his beard and Cossack hair. "Where the hell does she get her people?" Richard wonders as he lowers the window.

"You Montgomery?" Garth asks.

"Yes."

"Thought so, you fit the description." Garth replies laughing.

Richard is caught off guard by the comment. "What the fuck does that mean?" He asks himself.

"Before you enter," Garth says. "Here are the rules. They're pretty simple. You and your team's movements are restricted to the guest house, the front grounds only and the Humvee which you'll move from the main house to the guest house. You'll not be permitted to leave the grounds while you're working here. Any groceries or supplies you require, you'll provide a list to me. We order everything on-line and its delivered once a week. You miss something, you go without until the following week. Get me so far?"

"Hey, whatever it takes." Richard answers.

"I need a yes, or a no." Garth says grimacing at him.

"Jesus, yes, okay? Yes." He replies.

"You and your team will have no direct contact with anyone else on the premises unless we initiate it." Garth states. "Oh, and careful who you and your team communicate outside this location as we'll be monitoring everything."

There's no response from Richard. Garth stands there staring at him.

"Oh…yes, I understand." Richard finally replies

"One last thing, if you or your men break any of these rules I'll either slit your throat," Garth says as he extracts a very large Bowie knife from a sheath on the back of his belt and places its tip to Richard's throat. "Or I will gun you down, depending on my mood." As he pats the AK-47 slung over his shoulder. "Make sure you clearly convey this message to your team. Any questions or concerns?" He asks smiling as he re-sheaths his edged weapon.

Richard has a blank look on his now sheet white face. He's finding it difficult to even swallow. He tries to reply but his suddenly dry throat only permits him to nod his head in agreement.

"I need a verbal response please." Garth states.

"Yes." Richard replies in a whispered hoarse voice. Christ, the less contact he has with these people the better. He's already petrified of Reggie Byrnes and now he's completely intimidated by this freak. He's needs to get this assigned job done and get the hell out of here.

"Okay, proceed then. You'll head down this lane which leads to the curved driveway in front of the main house. The Humvee is parked in front and the keys are in the ignition. Take the access leading west after you pass the house and about two hundred yards down is the guest house. Park your vehicles in front of the garage. Your vehicles must be left out in the open at all times. Ms. Byrnes will contact you at her convenience to discuss what is expected of you. Have a pleasant day." Garth says snickering as he returns to the guardhouse through the side gate and opens the main gates.

Richard looks straight ahead as he enters and tries to ignore the warm wet sensation he felt in his pants when Garth placed the blade to his neck.

Garth calls Reggie. "There here. I gave him the ground rules." Garth says chuckling.

"How'd he take it?" Reggie asks.

"Just as you would expect." Garth replies.

Reggie giggles. "Thanks. I will have them up and running by nightfall. I have the Committee meeting before I can tend to them and then everyone should be off the hook for guard duty."

"Do what you have to do. I'm good until you get things worked out. I've had my fun for the day." Garth says.

"I'll let you know." Reggie says disconnecting the call.

"You two are so mean." Willow says smiling. "That man will forever be traumatized." Well aware of what Garth must have put him through.

"Don't worry; the damage was already done at Rainier, besides, I have a reputation to maintain." Reggie replies smirking.

"Evil woman, what persona do you use with the Committee?" Willow asks.

"A direct and straight forward professional who's willing to get her hands dirty…and right now, a nervous one." Reggie says taking a deep breath.

"Don't worry, you'll do great."

"I know but I still have butterflies. We only have one shot at this." Reggie says.

"Well, I leave you to get psyched up as I know the countdown is on. See you later and good luck." Willow says as she leaves Reggie's office.

Reggie sits and snacks away on a banana, then a yogurt followed by a few sips of bottled Perrier. She thinks and works better when she has something in her stomach. She completes a final review of the notes on her desk as she doesn't want to get tripped up on anything. These U.S. based Committee members are a highly intelligent group and many have died assuming less. They've not elevated themselves and so many others within their group to positions of such power and influence here and worldwide for so long, while still maintaining the secrecy of their very existence, by being careless. It's only through her capabilities and resources as a Handler has she been so successful in infiltrating their ranks while bringing Garth and Bertram along with her, through kinks in the Committee's armor she's discovered along the way. She hopes to do the same with Willow, Stogie and Oin and eventually other Handler teams until they can take full control of the reins of the Committee. It may be a far reaching goal but one her and Willow fully believe is attainable, more so now that they've teamed up. She takes a deep breath, its time and she accesses the highly secure site for the video conference call. Her screen immediately fills with a number of shadowed images; hers is the only one that's not camouflaged in any way.

"Ms. Byrnes," A male voice says and an associated shadowed image's snapshot illuminates as it speaks. "We are so glad you have joined us at the appointed time. Your predecessor was not so…diligent, shall we say. He had a more arrogant attitude."

"Thank you for having me and I'm sure you'll find me to be a very cooperative and respectful AR." Reggie replies. "But please, call me Reggie." She knows full well a man or a woman could be speaking as all the Members use voice altering software.

"We'll stick with Ms. Byrnes." The Male Voice answers.

"Of course." Reggie says.

"So, first you apprised us on the path of ruination Felix Belette was leading us down and now, it appears, you have a quashed a rebellion of sorts, including the removal of Mr. H's lab creation. An individual that was considered a high risk threat to the Committee…all done with the aid of a group you were fortunate to have present at your location." The Male Voice states with a touch of sarcasm and doubt.

"Yes, they're private contractors. I was fortunate to have worked with them while I was with the FBI. They had proved their worth assisting the bureau several times on various sensitive matters that were kept off the books. I believed they'd be quite beneficial in enhancing the security at this location and they had come down so I could discuss their participation." She answers.

"Why would you feel the need for that?" The Male Voice asks.

"As I had previously reported, there had been many lapses in Mr. Belette's judgment, so many, that with his passing, I believed it was time to take some precautionary measures and part of that was to update the security personnel by recruiting proven and trusted individuals who could provide a different perspective on procedures here where discretion is imperative. I believe you all have copies of the backgrounds of the three individuals I am referring to." Reggie says, involuntarily tapping her nails on the arm of her chair.

"Was there something amiss with Mr. Scott, the person who had been heading the security there for the past year? The same individual you had highly recommended to Mr. Belette for this role?" The Male Voice asks again, there's a tone of uncertainty in his words.

"Not at all. I had planned to put his unique talents to better use on Committee matters that required a highly skilled professional who could be tactful with his assignments." She replies.

"Give us a moment." The Male Voice says and immediately blocks Reggie from hearing any of the Members' internal conversations although she could see the various shadowed images light up as each Member voices their opinions. A couple minutes later the Male Voice comes back on-line.

"Ms. Byrnes, please enlighten us on the recent events at your location?" The Male Voice requests.

Reggie spends over an hour reporting her fictitious chain of events to the Committee Members, expanding on certain points she feels adds credence to her bogus tale. Her report is received uninterrupted and there is an eerie silence when she finishes.

"And what of the Orb?" The Male Voice finally asks.

"Unfortunately, at this point and time, I believe it remains in the possession of the Tsiatko." She answers.

"We have to ask, why did the Tsiatko not assist Frank Smirnov in this assault as they did at Rainier considering what was at risk for them and that he was, in theory, one of them?" The Male Voice says.

"In my opinion, at Rainier, the Tsiatko were simply defending their selves from Mr. Belette's ludicrous plan. I believe they have no interest in being the aggressor or exposing themselves any more than they need to." Reggie says. "Even if the life of Frank Smirnov was at stake."

There's another moment of quietness.

"Thank you, Ms. Byrnes for all your efforts. Continue with your agenda and, we will be monitoring your activity." The Male Voice says.

"I expect no less and I welcome any future input you may want to provide." Reggie replies and with that, her screen goes blank. She leans back in her chair, smiles and breathes a sigh of relief. She needs to update Willow and have a celebratory drink with her, with everyone and exits her office.

Beyond Reggie's now lifeless computer screen, the Committee Members' conversation continues. "Do we trust her?" One Member asks.

"Absolutely not. She's not as clever as she thinks." The Male Voice replies.

"Do we eliminate her then and if so, who replaces her?" Another Member asks.

"No, I strongly suggest we wait and see what she's up to." The Male Voice says.

"Why?" One other Member asks.

"We have time. I have someone on the inside to keep tabs on things." The Male Voice answers.

"Who?" A couple Members ask in unison.

"Let's just say he's someone she's recently brought back into the fold."

CHAPTER SIX

Frank enters the seemingly normal hallway of the bunker wing that contains the bedrooms. So far so good, nothing weird and he makes his way to the kitchen. As he enters the cookery he sees Oin, Gaylord and Zach exiting the living area.

"Hey," Zach calls smiling as he approaches Frank. "How you doing, you definitely were out of sorts last night, in a better mood?"

"Yea, I'm better." Frank lies. He's in no mood to share, not that he ever was, not is style.

Zach quickly checks behind him to make sure he's out of earshot of Gaylord and Oin. "Look, I know you're confined to quarters but let me bring you back some breakfast…we need to talk." He says in a hushed tone, a gleam in his eye.

Frank gives him a peevish look. "Not in the mood Zach. I don't have time to hear about another one of your schemes."

Zach looks back again to make sure the coast is clear and grabs Frank's arm. "Frank, neither of us like being under anyone's thumb and I know you have something up your sleeve." He whispers.

Frank shakes off Zach's grasp. "You know shit Zach." And turns away.

Zach walks backwards towards Oin and Gaylord pointing at Frank the whole time. "Bullshit Frank. Utter bullshit." He accuses.

Frank spins back around to face Zach, Oin and Gaylord. "And tell everyone to keep out today. I need solitude. I don't care who it is…Willow, Reggie, stay the fuck out of here." He demands before wheeling back around.

"What's that all about?" Oin asks.

"Just Frank being a fucking asshole," Zach replies. "Let's go." He grudgingly makes his way to the elevator with Oin on his tail, leaving Gaylord where he stands. Zach's jealous. Jealous that Frank not only has the Orb but unrestricted, no one knows what the hell he's doing or getting out of the Orb access. Zach grits his teeth hard thinking about it as they ride the elevator up. He knows he himself could have done shit with the Orb…it's just, it's killing him not knowing what Frank is doing with it…or what it's doing to him. Zach's edge with the Committee and with Frank has been what he knows and now he feels he's losing that. That's why he's stuck around, to learn everything he can but he's feeling too much like a pawn. One that's being controlled by Reggie and he doesn't like it. He needs to cut and run soon.

"I'm starving," Oin says as the elevator doors open. "I'm glad Willow and Reggie told us about the food, I can't wait to dig in."

"Huh? Oh yeah, me too." Zach says faking interest. He knows he has to appear cooperative, keep faking he's out of options even though he never is. As the elevator doors close behind him, Zach hopes he'll learn something of value from everyone's chit chat over breakfast that'll help get him the hell out of here in one piece and with some idea of what his next plausible course of action should be.

Gaylord approaches Frank in the kitchen. "And me, my brother, do you need me to leave?" He asks.

"I do." Frank says. "Only for a short while, I need time alone. My mind is… conflicted."

"As you wish, I will be back later." And with that Gaylord is gone.

Frank knows Gaylord is not offended in any way. The Tsiatko are practical, take everything at face value and do not have the same emotional sensitivity as humans do. He makes coffee, electing to stand and watch as the carafe fills, letting the aroma of the strong brew penetrate his nostrils. He pours a large mug full of the steaming beverage, adding cane sugar and a good helping of evaporated milk as he anticipates the taste of the rejuvenating elixir. He loves his coffee in the morning. He pivots to the island to find…Ivan and Dasha before him; busy chatting while filling their plates from a bountiful spread of buttered potato pancakes, grilled seasoned potatoes and eggs fried in bacon grease along with thick slabs of crisp bacon set out on the counter top. There's a heaping plate of thick slices of toasted homemade bread and an assortment of jars containing fresh made jams scattered about amongst a small jug of real maple syrup and a bowl of fresh sour cream. The tantalizing smell of the banquet is overpowering.

"Are you hungry?" Dasha asks, handing him a plate.

Frank doesn't fight it. He decides to let it happen, observe, absorb and try to figure it all out.

"I am." He answers calmly, taking the plate and sitting down in the process. What's throwing him off is that he's not reliving a memory from the past and his grandparents definitely seem to be in the here and now. He begins to fill his own platter, the food is as real as it can get and he wolfs down a slice of salty smoked bacon…well if that's hallucinated food, bring it on.

"Did you sleep well?" Dasha asks.

"Reasonably," He answers. He hesitates before continuing. "I could have sworn you were in my room grandpa."

Ivan looks up from his plate. "I was checking on you and trying to get our message across."

Frank takes a big gulp of coffee to help wash down the bacon. "The message?" He asks.

"The Orb has many secrets." Ivan states.

"You know about the Orb?" Frank says a bit astonished.

"We know about a lot of things." Ivan says as he props his elbows on the table and intertwines his hands as if in prayer. "That's why you need to come see us."

Frank smiles. "But I can see you now."

"No," Dasha says placing a hand on his arm. He can feel it as if it's the real thing. "We mean you need to come home."

"Why?" Franks asks.

Ivan waves off his question. "You first need to learn more first." He says.

"From the Orb?" Frank asks, looking for confirmation.

Ivan doesn't confirm Frank's question. "Frank, knowing and understanding aren't the same thing but, they are intertwined." Ivan replies.

Frank smiles, this statement sounds like one of the many sayings Frank has heard come from his grandpa's lips before…another riddle about life.

"That's what your real purpose is and when you're done, well…you WILL know and understand all that is meant to be." Ivan emphasizes as he takes hold of Dasha's hand.

Frank has so many questions but doesn't want to push things, he reaches for another slice of toast and when he turns back…his grandparents are gone. The evidence of their visit clearly remains via the feast of food that still lies before him. Frank accepts their disappearance with the same calm demeanor he tried to accept their appearance. He continues to eat not wanting the well prepared meal to go to waste, trying to make sense of what has just happened and questions whether their confession of knowing…whatever that may be, is true or whether this was a hallucination, a continuing side affect of his interaction with the Orb. Again, he tries to determine whether this interaction was real or reality and mulls how he could possibly explain this concept, he's beginning to understand so well, to another. He returns to the coffee maker and fills his mug. It's time for the Orb and decides to complete this day's enlightenment in the quiet and solitude of the bedroom where the Orb is tucked away waiting for him, maybe pining to reveal who knows what. As he heads to the hallway, he pauses to look back at the kitchen…the spread is gone. There are only remnants of coffee in the pot as proof that he was actually in there but nothing to confirm his grandparents were at all. However, his stomach is clearly full and, as he looks down, he sees an egg yolk stain on the front of his shirt. There's even residue of bacon grease on his fingers which he wipes off on the side of his jeans…this is getting fucked up.

Frank trusts he'll be left alone as he requested but reminds himself of Zach's past shady intentions so he not only locks the bedroom door but props a chair under the knob so that any human unwelcome entry will be next to impossible. He lies on the bed and checks the travel alarm clock on the night stand; it's ten am. He un-wraps the Orb and puts it on his chest, holding it in place with crossed arms. He closes his eyes and opens his mind and body to all that the Orb is willing to concede. He's suddenly shocked out of the deep vegetated like state he's in by a sense of intrusion. He opens his eyes and moves the Orb to the side as he sits up, still in a semi hypnotic like trance. He glances at the clock; it's now seven-thirty in the evening, nine and a half hours have fleeted by. He squeezes his eyes open and shut, hoping to bring them into focus as he rises to check the door. Gaylord is silently standing there, watching, guarding.

"How long have you been there?" Frank asks.

"All the while my brother." He answers.

Frank switches on a light so he can clearly see Gaylord's face. "And what have you seen?" Frank asks.

"I have only seen you." Gaylord answers.

"And was there anything for me to be concerned about?" Frank inquires.

"I can sense a change in you my brother, with each time you become one with that device." Gaylord says. "More so now."

"A change for better or worse?"

"It depends on whose perspective you are viewing it from." Gaylord replies.

"I'm not sure about your answer. Are you taking lessons from Brother?" Frank says.

"I do not understand." Gaylord replies.

Frank shakes his head. "How do you see it?" He asks.

"It is as it should be." Gaylord states.

Frank chuckles and lets that obligatory answer sink in. "I agree. Then it's time…time for me to go home." He confirms.

CHAPTER SEVEN

Zach has learned shit over breakfast and is feeling frustrated as he's left with no choice but to kill time. They're all killing time actually, with the Handlers anxiously waiting for Reggie to finish her big meeting with the Committee…hoping for confirmation of the "in" that they have planned so hard for. With that, they believe they can take the next big step in assuming control of the Committee itself and thwart their efforts to abandon this world to begin anew on another planet…just the Committee members and their inner fold, leaving the remaining occupants on this planet to suffer a slow, painful death. Ah, such high hopes these Handlers have and willing to make such sacrifices to save Earth and all who reside here…too bad it will all be for not. He knows first-hand the Committee doesn't let you slide in this easy. You need to have something they want or have to go through a lot more proving ground then Reggie or the rest of the Handlers have. Handlers or not, they'll feel the fury of the Committee, Zach knows this.

Reggie struts into the room, her face beaming. "We did it." She announces, displaying a lot less emotion than Zach would have expected.

"They bought it?" Willow asks.

"I'm confident they did." Reggie replies.

Willow claps her hands. "Another step in the right direction." She says.

Zach is a bit surprised that the reaction from the Handlers is so low key, just smiles and nods of approval, nothing over the top. To him, this is a very controlled group. He guesses age, experience and numerous failed attempts will have that affect.

"And we are going to do something I'm sure none of us have done in quite some time, we're going to celebrate this victory, regardless of how small it is."

Reggie says before turning to Zach. "I know I've been rough on you and I'm sure you feel like an outcast, I'm not apologizing for my actions but, you're welcome to join us and…it would mean a lot to me if you did." She lies.

Zach's caught off guard by the offer and stands to face her. "Of course, it would be my privilege." He answers cautiously, the fox in the hen house look reignited in his eyes and he's a bit confounded by the slight smirk that appears on Willow's face when she hears him accept the invitation. As much as Willow dislikes Zach, she understands Reggie's game…part of which is to keep him close and under their watchful eye and then, after tonight, it's one less thing to worry about.

"Thank you." Reggie replies smiling. "Bertram, find us some bottles of champagne but give me a bit before we pop the corks. I have to meet with Montgomery's group and get our new security detail on track first. After that, we're having a little soiree."

"Hang on Bertram." Zach says. "Let me help." Of course he'll celebrate with them…what better way to pry information than from those who've had a little too much of the bubbly stuff. He might get what he wants and needs after all. As he walks out with Bertram, he looks back at Reggie and experiences a slight pang of guilt; he's going to hate seeing her go down. Regardless of the circumstances, he's going to miss her.

Reggie heads to the guest house to meet with Montgomery. She's smiling and shaking her head along the way, she has Zach on her mind. She knows he's not worth the trouble and she should put him down like a rabid dog, as the saying goes, but she can't. They have a history, not that it really means anything to her… he's alive simply because he hasn't fulfilled his purpose for being here. She giggles knowing he's up to no good and she's sure his plan tonight is take advantage of anyone who's had too much and try to extract whatever he can but, two can play that game. She raps on the guest house door before entering. "Gentlemen," She calls out as she walks in. "You three," She says, indicating the pilots lounging in the TV room. "Stay right where you are and enjoy yourselves, it's your boss I came to see." She continues toward the kitchen nodding to Montgomery to follow. She opens the fridge and grabs a bottle of carbonated water, taking a drink of the refreshing liquid before she leans back on the counter. Montgomery scampers in. "A little quieter in here since we're discussing business." She says. She looks at her bottle. "Oh, you want one?"

"No, I'm good." Montgomery answers, holding up an opened half bottle of beer.

Reggie takes another sip of Pellegrino. "You and your men aren't indulging in that stuff too much are you? I need at least one of you with your mind fresh and clear at all times."

"No ma'am. We know our job."

"Yes, I trust you do, otherwise I wouldn't have you here." Reggie replies, a steely look on her face.

"How soon do you need us to start?"

"As soon as we're done our little chit chat." Reggie answers.

"Down to business then," Montgomery says. "Are you worried about entries or exits?"

Reggie smiles. "Entries."

"How many people are on site?"

"That doesn't concern you." Reggie says.

"It will make my job easier."

"Just don't rock the boat and your job will be easier, understand?"

Montgomery nods his agreement. "And the Tsiatko?" He asks.

"What about them?"

"I'm sure it isn't a coincidence this place is where it is. I mean there's a sign just up the road at Willow Creek that says — Gateway to Bigfoot Country."

"You noticed that did you?" Reggie says as she starts to tap her nails on the counter top.

"Yea, it caught my eye. After what happened at Rainier something like that would get my attention." Montgomery answers, taking another swig of his beer.

"You don't have to worry about them." Reggie answers.

"Worry? Are you kidding me? We can't pick track those things, not with video or infrared. If they come looking, we're dead meat." Montgomery answers emptying his bottle and pulls another from an open case on the counter.

Reggie's tapping gets a little more rhythmic. She says nothing, simply watches as Montgomery gets increasingly more nervous.

"Please tell me we're not here to defend against those things." He pleads.

Her tapping stops. "You're not. I only want to ensure we're not intruded upon, not that we are expecting anyone or anything. By going this route, with your team covering the security, it restricts the amount of personnel we require on site to accomplish that task. That's all that's to it." Reggie explains truthfully. "Feel better?"

Montgomery wipes away the perspiration that has been building on his forehead. "Yea, yea, I'm good with that."

"You're making me nervous." Reggie says. "Questioning if I made a mistake bringing you back on board."

"We'll do the job, ma'am. I guess I'm still a bit…shaky, about…you know…those guys we lost. They were tough, experienced men and they were…wiped out, just like that." Montgomery says, snapping his fingers as he takes a deep breath trying to get the memories of that event out of his head.

"Look," Reggie says. "I don't want to sound like a bitch but those guys made the wrong play, got cocky, went where they knew they shouldn't have and paid the price. Simply put, don't do anything stupid and you'll be fine. Got it?"

"Sorry, yea, I got it."

"Now going back to your earlier comment, you said you can't pick them up at all but what about the video in Rainier there when they were shown with Allmass and Smirnov?" Reggie says.

"Who?" Montgomery asks. The names aren't hitting home.

"The two guys in the cavern that were standing in front of the Tsiatko." Reggie clarifies.

"Oh…those two. All we got on tape was the shape of the Tsiatko in the background, nothing more and I think we only got that because they let us, they were helping Allmass and Smirnov show off for whomever those two were trying to piss off, which I believe was Belette. Otherwise, nothing picks those things up, not even radar. Normally most electronics shut down whenever they're present… well, that's the theory." Montgomery says.

"I'm well aware of the many hypothesize." She feels like testing those theories against Gaylord but that would be pushing things too far. "Any other pertinent questions then or are we done here?" She asks.

"How long is this job?"

"Do you need to be somewhere?"

"No disrespect but to be honest, I'd rather be anywhere but here. Since it was you who made the request, I really didn't believe I had a choice. If I had said no, I think I'd be face down in a hole right about now." Montgomery states.

Reggie smirks and walks for the door. "I'll let you know when I'm done with you." She replies. "Good night boys." She says to the vegging pilots in passing.

"Your day is going to come." Montgomery mumbles as Reggie closes the door behind her. "And sooner than you think." He moves into the TV room. "Guys, I'm going to take the first shift."

"You sure boss?" One of the pilots asks.

"Positive. I need to test the equipment and get a feel for the place first hand to make sure we get everything covered. You guys take it easy tonight. Don't worry; you're going get more time in than you care to."

"Thanks." Another answers.

Montgomery grabs his coat and the keys for the SUV and heads outside. He pops open its rear hatch and extracts from a case, one of the high tech drones they brought, similar to the ones they used at Rainier. They're shaped like a dragonfly but are the size of a small rat with thermal sensors, night visions and live audio/video feed but Montgomery has added another special little feature this time, high tech microphones. These drones are now equipped with match-stick size sensors that can pin point, record and transmit live conversations from up to a hundred feet away, the latest in military grade technology. Something special he didn't share with Ms. Byrnes. "It's time to have some fun." He says as he preps it for flight.

Reggie makes one more stop before she heads to the party. When she arrives, everyone is milling around and their mood is jovial. As promised, they haven't opened the bottles of champagne but there's a bucket of ice and a bottle of aged bourbon already half empty. Several plates of assorted hors d'oeuvres are out, pulled from the reserve of food kept in the commercial fridges and freezers in the main kitchen. It seems they're taking this celebration seriously.

Garth approaches her, his lock swaying with each stride and hands her a chilled bottle of Don Perignon along with a small hand towel. "The honor is yours." He says.

Without hesitation she removes the wire cage, covers the cork with the towel, gives it a firm twist, followed by a slight downward pressure and the cork pops without incident. There's a round of applause for her successful effort. She walks to the table and fills an assortment of flutes already placed out. She waits until everyone has a glass. "A toast...to us, to our success and soon, to a better and changed world." There's a clinking of glasses followed by a response of "To us!" It's obvious to her that the alcohol has put everyone in a more relaxed spirit. She takes a seat near the food and munches as she sips her drink. She watches Zach already moving about obviously trying to pry information. He may think he's being subtle but he's not, all the Handlers are aware and on their guard. As he unsuccessfully works the room, he keeps glancing Reggie's way, finally making his way over and pulls up a chair beside her.

"Can I top up your drink?" He asks.

She looks down at her glass and at his nearly empty highball of bourbon. "You know what, I feel like having bourbon myself. Why don't you sit here and I'll get one for myself and refresh yours at the same time." Standing and grabbing his glass before he can even respond.

"Won't argue with that." He says as she heads for the makeshift bar that's been set up.

Moments later Reggie returns with the bourbons and takes her seat. "Cheers." She says raising her glass. Zach raises his in response and the match is on. Who's going to get what information first? Willow watches intently from across the room. About fifteen minutes later, Reggie waves her over to join them. She does willingly and in no time, with the drinks continuing, the conversation becomes vigorous. An hour and a half later, Zach is slumped on the table, out of it. Without prompting, Garth and Stogie come over and take Zach to his room to sleep things off.

"That was easier than I thought it would be." Willow remarks.

Reggie sets an empty vial on the table and laughs. She had taken an early advantage and added a dose of Sodium Thiopental to Zach's drinks that she and the others had graciously served him. The recipient of this drug becomes more talkative and less inhibited as it affects the cortex, the decision making region of the brain. It also distorts short term memory so Zach will have forgotten most of what he discussed while under its control. She waits for Garth and Stogie's return and with that, all the Handlers take a seat at the table.

"You think he's out for the night?" Willow asks.

Garth looks at Stogie for confirmation,. "Yea, we're sure." Garth says.

"Did you get everything we need from him?" Oin asks.

Willow and Reggie smile. "That and a little more." Willow says laughing.

Reggie gives Willow a friendly push. "Maybe more than Willow needed to hear." She says blushing.

"So, things are still on track?" Bertram asks, he's still apprehensive about the next stage. He wants to know things are progressing but he hopes not too fast, he's not sure he's ready.

Reggie senses his anxiety and gives him a reassuring look. "It's all good. We got enough out of Zach to give us solid leads on where all the Committee members here in the states are located."

Willow pushes a list across the table to Stogie. "We wrote it all the pertinent stuff down while you were hauling Zach away. You think this is enough details to work with?"

Stogie examines the paper and pulls the cigar from his mouth. "Yea…with our technology, it won't matter what firewalls they've put up or cloaking software they used during Reggie's meeting with them, with this info…I can track them down."

"How long will it take?" Oin asks. Like Bertram, he's feeling anxious about what's in store.

Stogie is chomping on the cigar now thinking about the time line. "It's not going to happen overnight and there's quite a few of them…three days, maybe four for all of them. I can probably have the first one or two by end of the day tomorrow." He answers.

"That soon?" Bertram exclaims.

"Yea, that soon." Garth pipes in. "Don't be a shit about this, it's not like it's a surprise, we've been planning this long enough."

"I know, I know." Bertram replies leaning back in his chair, removing his bow-tie and unbuttoning the top button of his shirt. "Look, I need to come clean with you all. To be honest, I wasn't aiming too hard when we took out those guys in the bunker, I didn't hit anybody…sorry but I'm not comfortable with killing. And now, to be an actual part of an assassin team, taking out Committee members, possibly even women," He buries his head in his hands for a moment and rubs his face before facing everyone again. " I'm just worried I'll let you all down and screw this up."

Oin, surprising everyone, takes the lead and reaches across Garth and firmly grabs Bertram by his jacket sleeve, yanking him across Garth's lap so he can look him face to face. "Seriously? To be upfront with you, fuck off with that attitude!" And he shoves Bertram back into his seat. "I don't like what's next any better than you do but as sure as shit, I'm not going through another couple hundred more years of this same crap." He looks around the table. "Like all of us have for the last too damn long, just to end up back in the same friggin place. I've had a taste of getting involved and trying to actually make a difference, not just push gently from the sidelines and, you know what? It felt good to be doing something regardless if a few, or a whole fucking lot of people got in the way. I don't swear, I don't like it, I feel it's beneath me to do so but screw it…I need to make a point here and Goddamn it, at times those are the only words to help get the message across. So quit being a pussy and let's get this job done!" Oin sees the rest of the Handlers are a gawk of his outburst. "And, unlike most of you, I don't mind Zach…I like the guy actually but if he has to be the fall guy, so be it. I'm not going to lose any sleep over it." He takes a shot of bourbon from his glass and leans back in his chair, folding his arms across his chest. "Sorry, I'll shut up now."

Garth Scott applauds Oin's spiel and there are only silent gestures of agreement from the others. Bertram nods his acceptance as well. "Do you think Zach suspects anything?" Garth asks.

"Not a bit." Reggie says. "The smug bas…" She holds back. "I'm positive Zach thinks he was nothing more than bait to get Frank here and that we intended to ply him for every bit of information on the Committee to ensure our plan's success. He's right to a certain degree, there was specific intelligence we did require from him, but as of tonight we have what we need and he has no idea that he gave it up. And while he's here, he hopes he'll find out whatever he believes he needs for his salvation, his greed, his own self interests, not suspecting the real reason for the charade was to set him up as our patsy. " She has a sour dejected look at her face as the last of those words escape her lips…at one time, an earlier time, she had hoped for more from him.

Willow intercedes. "Bertram, yes, we are now officially assassins and murderers but we always were, now we're just more hands on, that's the commitment we've all voluntarily made. Live with it." She says matter of factly. "And hopefully by week's end, the Committee Members we've targeted will be eliminated. They won't know what happened until its too late. One of their faults lies with the fact they are Committee Members, gone for days at a time without accountability to no one. As we take them down one by one, we'll make sure there's no trace of their bodies to give warning to anyone else. And when it is all said and done, we'll put the entire blame on Zach, the former elite associate of the Committee. The man who lied about his secret plan with Belette to take down the insurgency… his real agenda was to kill the Committee members to ensure his own survival. And as we'll explain to the International Committee members, the reason for his treacherous actions was that he believed the plan to vacate this world would never get off the ground and he didn't want to be looking over his shoulder for the rest of his life."

"So, while the four of you go after the Members, we'll keep Zach here with no real alibi." Reggie adds. "When the time comes, we'll deny he was here during the time of the Committee Members' slayings; that he ran off. We feed him to the wolves, the wolves being us because as the official AR of the Committee here, I should be able to step in to take over the U.S. operations."

"And who puts him down?" Oin asks.

"I will." Willow interjects before Reggie can even contemplate an answer.

"What about Montgomery's crew?" Garth asks. "They're monitoring the property, what if they see Zach or get him on tape?"

"First, I'm going to restrict Zach's movements, put him under house arrest for use of a better term, to minimize the risk." Reggie answers. "And if Montgomery accidently picks something up, I'll handle it. I've got him under my thumb." No one responds. Everyone is running everything through their heads. There's a lot at risk and their breaking new ground as Handlers.

Willow breaks the quietude. "We all good now that we talked it through again?"

There's an assortment of nods and murmurs of affirmation. 'I don't know about the rest of you, but I need another drink." Bertram says and heads for the bar. The rest of the Handlers let him be, leaving him to boost his courage or drown his doubts.

Zach is out, unaware of the world around him even though he's being shaken quite violently. "For fuck's sake, tonight would be the night you get hammered." Frank loudly whispers, scolding an incoherent Zach. He's been trying to awaken and determine if he has an obliging Zach to aide him for a few minutes now, but he's having no success. "Goddamn it." He mutters, grabbing Zach by his shirt and pulling him upright. He swings Zach's feet off the bed and bends down hoisting him over his shoulder. Frank grunts as the full dead weight of Zach hits him. He gently opens the bedroom door to check the hallway before heading for the back stairs to haul Zach off to the bunker. Frank's beginning to regret not asking for Gaylord's assistance with this.

Once on the grounds and Frank moving quicker, Zach's being jostled hard enough to finally jar him awake even though he's in a deep fog and his body feels lifeless. "What the hell? Whoever you are and wherever you're taking me…I'm warning you, if you don't put me down right now… I'm going to puke all over you." He slurs out.

"It's me, Frank! Now shut up, we're going on a trip." Frank answers glancing back at the mansion as he progresses towards the bunker.

Zach recognizes Frank's voice and gives his head a shake. "Put me down or else I'm going to heave." Zach warns as he pushes against Frank's back almost toppling them both. Frank drops him hard on the ground and it knocks the air out of Zach. Zach groans, catches his breath and props himself up. "A trip, a trip where?' He mutters.

"I'll explain but we can't sit out here in the open. C'mon, we have to keep going." Frank says as he grabs Zach's arm, pulling him upright and throwing it around his shoulder for support. "We're going back home to Lanesboro." Frank answers as they continue on.

"To Minnesota? Christ, what for? You haven't been there since your grandparents died." A slightly more alert Zach asks.

"I got an invitation." Frank states.

Montgomery has been busy. Busy videotaping the entire exchange among the festive group of Handlers as his remote controlled drone hangs sixty feet outside the window of the celebration room, concealed in the dark of the night. He has no idea its Handlers he's recording, to him they're mutineers and he's captured every word. His attention is distracted by movement the infrared sensors have picked up and he flies over to monitor two individuals leaving the main house. He silently follows them, staying high so the drone doesn't attract their attention. He hovers over them as they stop to have words. He's too high up to pick up their discussion but zooms in with the camera to try to identify them. He stares into the screen as the distant images come into focus. "Holy shit!" He exclaims once he recognizes who the pair are. He monitors them as far as he can, which is to the entrance of the secret bunker hidden among a dense grove of fir and pine trees. He sits back in his pilot seat, the drone's operation the last think on his mind. "What the hell is going on here?"

CHAPTER EIGHT

Frank and Zach take the elevator down to the living quarters. Zach is woozy but is able to move without any aid. "Why tonight of all nights did you decide to get drunk?" Frank asks in frustration.

"I had three drinks, that's it. I know what I can handle." Zach replies taking a seat on the couch, resting back.

Frank leans against the entranceway. "What do you remember?" He says

Zach massages his temples, shifting his eyes back and forth, trying to recall. "I remember partying with them…then sitting and talking with Reggie when she returned…Willow joined us, which was strange, I know she hates me. After that, nothing, it's a fuzzy blank." He says. He sits forward as it hits home. "Those mothers…they drugged me."

"Why?" Frank asks.

Zach pushes back his hanging hair with his hands. "Ugh…no fucking idea."

"It doesn't matter. We're getting out of here." Franks says.

"Why to Lanesboro?" Zach asks.

"Because, there's something there I have to check out." Frank replies.

"Okay, that tells me a lot."

"Look, you want to come along or stay here?"

"Hey, I'm in." Zach answers.

"I'm going to need all the files you have, everything you showed me in San Francisco and Mr. H's journals. Is that a problem?"

"Why?" Zach asks. "Just ask me what you need to know?"

Frank turns, placing his back against the wall to face Zach better. "I need to go through them first hand. Is that going to be an issue?"

Zach contemplates Frank's request. "No, not at all. What's in there is old news now. We're way past what I thought was important back then; not that back then was so long ago, so much has happened so fast."

"Tell me about it." Frank says. "How much money do you have?"

Zach digs out his cash. "About a grand." He says as he's counting it.

"A grand?" Frank asks.

"What? I don't like to go light. Why?"

"We need travel money and I only have a couple hundred." Frank answers.

"I've got nothing other than what I'm wearing." Zach says.

"Don't worry about that. We're going to bus it to San Francisco where I have a storage unit. We'll supply up, pick up those papers wherever you've stashed them and then we're off to Lanesboro." Frank says.

"I don't know if we have that much time to hike it there. It has to be fifteen miles to nearest town. They'll know we're gone before we even get there?"

"Gaylord!" Frank calls out and momentarily he enters. "Gaylord has arranged for a few of our brethren to haul us to Willow Creek. There's buses running all night from there to Arcata and then it's a direct ride to Frisco."

Zach knows these beasts have a full gait of thirty-five miles per hour. It'll only be a twenty minute ride cross country. "Frank, you should know they have a drone unit monitoring the grounds. The same one that was at Rainier." Zach announces.

"We'll be leaving through the back door." Frank says.

"What back door?" Zach asks.

Frank grins.

Crap, Zach knows what's coming. He's not a fan of that merging stuff.

"Ready?" Franks asks.

Zach stands. "No." And they head back up to the bunker's garage where their rides are waiting. Frank and Zach have time before the three a.m. bus leaves Willow Creek for Arcata so they grab something to eat and drink from the vending machines. To be on the safe side they split up to eat and wait while they're hanging in the passenger lounge for the bus's departure, it's only a forty minute ride to Arcata and then a seven hour direct to San Francisco, not bad. They discover there's a surprising number of night time travelers which is for the better, they'll blend into a crowd easier and in a short time, boarding for the bus is announced and they decide to stay separated, taking seats at opposite ends of the Greyhound.

It moves out and Frank reclines the seat hoping to have a short nap along the way to Arcata before they change buses. As they pull out on to the highway, Frank reads the billboard at the town's perimeter. "Willow Creek - Gateway to Bigfoot Country". The sign gives Frank a sense of assurance and he dozes off. They quickly arrive in Arcata; Frank's nap feels like it lasted seconds. The transfer of buses is quick with Frank and Zach staying separate. Frank finds a solitary spot in the very back and is quickly asleep again. His slumber is an erratic one filled with images of his grandparents, the Orb and events that may yet come. He is woken from his deep slumber by the jolt of the bus coming to a hard stop at the Union Square Hilton in San Francisco and he patiently waits for all those in front of him to disembark. He steps off the bus and stretches. The view of this urban center, especially this section of the city centre brings back pangs of pain for her…his jewel, the one he so violently avenged. Part of him wants to head to her apartment but he knows he can't. That chapter of his life is over and done with; it's no use revisiting it.

Zach approaches him. "Where to now?" He asks.

"A storage center on Brannan Street. It's only about a mile and a half from here so we'll walk." Frank replies.

"Works for me. Wouldn't mind getting the kinks out of my legs." Zach says. They tread in silence, keeping their heads down as they've both spent substantial time here. Forty-five minutes later they arrive and Frank leads the way into his storage unit, switching on a light. Zach follows closing the door behind him. "Holy crap Frank, what are you expecting a war?" Zach says looking at the visible array of weapons and supplies. He wonders how many people have storage units set up across the U.S. just like this…hundreds if not thousands and he's sure this isn't the only one Frank has. This country is a crazy and dangerous place.

"I like to be prepared." Frank replies. "Load up what you think you'll need, there's duffle bags over there." Indicating a corner of the unit. "In the back cupboards, there're clothes that should fit you." Frank opens a side cabinet, pulls out a couple bundles of one hundred dollar U.S bills, a number of alias credit cards, a couple designer wallets, two burner phones, a couple passports along with a medical kit and tosses them in a sports bag, followed by a few clothes from the cupboard. He strips off what's he's wearing, throws them in a trash bag and puts on tan cargo pants and a black t-shirt as well as fresh socks and military style boots. He puts on a shoulder holster, threads an ISIS -2 silencer on a Glock 19 and slides it in along with two loaded clips and tosses on a black flight jacket before filling a duffle bag with assorted weaponry and ammo. Zach watches in amazement at Frank's efficiency in these tasks. He's done in minutes. Frank drops his filled duffle bag by the door and picks up the loaded sports bag. "I'll be back in half an hour. I'm going to get us a vehicle." And leaves before Zach can reply. Thirty minutes later, Zach hears a vehicle pull up. It's Frank in a black SUV and Zach can see by the license plate that it's a rental. Zach, now attired in clothes similar to Frank, loads his and Frank's duffle bags in the back while Frank grabs the garbage bag of clothes and tosses them in a bin a few units down. Frank locks the storage unit and they both climb in the vehicle.

"Where to?" Frank asks.

"Glenford, Ohio." Zach replies.

"Ohio?"

Yea, Ohio." Zach states.

"Hang on." Frank says exiting the SUV and returning to the storage unit. He comes back with a couple of sleeping bags and tosses them in the back seat. "It's going to be a driving marathon so we may as well sleep as comfortably as we can." He throws the vehicle in gear and they hit the road.

CHAPTER NINE

Oin comes bursting into the kitchen. He stops, surveying who's all present. "Shit…Zach's not in his room! Has anyone seen him?!" He demands. They all look at each other but there are only blank looks and negative responses.

"I thought he'd be sleeping it off." Stogie says amazed.

"And the bunker?" Willow asks.

"Not yet, thought I'd check here first." Oin replies.

"Reggie and I will check the bunker. Frank seems to be getting a little erratic as to who shows up there." Willow says. "The rest of you check the house and the grounds."

"If need be, I'll see if Montgomery's team spotted anything but I really don't want to unless it's absolutely necessary!" Reggie calls out as they all go their separate directions. As Reggie and Willow make their way to the bunker, they scan the skyline and spot a drone on patrol. The drone veers their way but Reggie waves it off. They enter a much quieter bunker this time. There's no blaring TV, no aroma of fresh coffee in the kitchen, nothing. They search every wing, starting with the bedroom one. They check the bedroom Frank was in first and see the Orb glowing, still tucked away between the pillows where they saw it the last time. As they turn to leave, they are startling by Gaylord, who's standing in the hallway.

"Gaylord, where is Frank?" Willow asks.

"I do not know." He answers.

"Would you tell me if you did?" She asks.

"I would not." He replies.

"I thought as much. Why are you here then if Frank isn't?" Willow inquires.

"I am here because the Orb is here." Gaylord says.

"Of course, after all, Frank is the trusting kind." Willow replies sharply and sarcastically as she and Reggie push past him. They abandon their plan to search the rest of the bunker and instead head up to ground level so Reggie can call Montgomery.

"Montgomery." He answers.

"Did your team spot any activity on the grounds last night?" Reggie asks.

Montgomery smiles. "Nothing, all was quiet." He lies. "Why?"

"Just checking." Reggie replies. "I thought I saw movement from the windows late in the night."

"I was on patrol myself and I can assure you, nothing caught my eye. Do you want to view the tapes?" Montgomery offers hoping she doesn't call his bluff.

'No, that's fine." She answers. "Thanks." And ends the call.

"And?" Willow asks.

"Nothing." Reggie answers.

Willow calls Stogie. "Anything?" She asks.

"Nada." Stogie answers.

"No luck on our end either." She says hanging up. They're both unsure of what to make of it all.

"Well," Reggie says. "We won't have to lie about not knowing Zach's whereabouts."

"Do you think he heard us?"

"No," Reggie replies. "I think this has nothing to do with last night, we continue as planned. Any thoughts on Frank?"

"I'm not sure why he left," Willow says giving her head a slight shake. "Or his reason for taking Zach with him but I do know this," As she looks Reggie in the eyes. "He left the Orb behind which can mean only one thing…he's coming back."

CHAPTER TEN

Frank and Zach take the 505 to Sacramento and from there onto the I-80 East which will be the main drag they'll be on for most of the trip to Glenford. There's little said between the two of them as Frank's mind is occupied with thoughts about the paths his life has taken, or rather been directed, and where he's going to end up in this massive cluster fuck of events. Him and is Fate….his Power he has had so much faith in for so long, that he's learned to rely on to lead him. He wonders now if it actually exists or whether he's had this false belief in something that never was… the one thing he's trusted for so long. As he drives, he keeps glancing in the rear view mirror, half expecting his grandparents to appear in the back seat at any moment.

Zach can't help but notice Frank's actions and turns to look out the rear window of the SUV. "Are we being followed?" Zach asks unknowingly interrupting Frank's introspection.

"Huh? No." Frank replies. "Should we be?"

"You keep checking the mirror."

"Oh, force of habit." Frank lies. "We're good." He watches Zach intermittently as Zach's attention is fixated out the side window, wondering if he's able to trust that Zach will turn over everything he's got stashed. "Why Glenford for hiding the papers?" He asks.

Zach doesn't turn his way, just answers into the window. "Small village, no big city surveillance, no ties to me and the bank's building was declared a historic site so no fear of it closing or being knocked down."

Frank nods in agreement with this logic.

"Why the sudden hard on for the papers?" Zach asks.

Frank glances at Zach. "My gut tells me there's something important buried in them."

"Like what?"

"No idea, not even sure I'll find anything."

"So who came up with this train of thought, you or Willow?" Zach asks.

Frank understands where this question is coming from…is he being led or is this something all his own. "It's all me." He answers.

Zach turns to him. "You sure?"

Frank glances at him quickly again. "Yea." Frank lies once more; not interested in trying to explain the appearance of his grandparents in the bunker and how interactions with them brought on this decision. Zach says nothing and directs his attention back to his window. They drive almost constantly, switching driving duties as one or the other tires, each taking turns sleeping in the back. At first they only temporarily halt their journey to eat as they need or to fuel up but they do make the time to freshen up with a shower at a truck stop half way along the route as neither of them wants to feel like they did after their detained stay in the caverns of Mt. Rainier. For Frank, the shower is a welcome relief and does cause him to laugh as he soaps up under the steaming hot water reliving the memory of Oin and Gaylord getting stoned in the back of Oin's van the last time they made a similar stop near Seattle.

"Thinking about Gaylord and Oin I bet!" Zach shouts from the adjoining stall hearing Frank's unprovoked laughter. "I was doing the same thing."

"Crazy times!" Frank yells back.

A quick meal later and it's Zach's turn behind the wheel as they continue on and as Frank sleeps in the back, the quiet and isolation gives Zach the opportunity to contemplate how screwed up his well laid plans have become since he came across Frank working as a Deputy Sheriff at Mt. Rainier. He was riding high back then, now…he's at the bottom of the barrel. He shakes his head wondering how he managed to fall such a long way in such a very short time. The bible quote "The Nephilim were on the earth in those days — and also afterwards — when the sons of God went in to the daughters of humans, who bore beautiful children to them. These were the heroes that were of old, warriors of renown." pops into his head. The very quote that obsessed him as a child and inspired him to create his own theories on the Tsiatko, the belief in their existence and how that ultimately led him to the Committee and his reincarnation from Adam Pope to Zachariah Allmass. Maybe reincarnation is not the right description since he did sell his soul to the Committee; it no longer seemed to exist in Zachariah Allmass, well, maybe. He has so many regrets now. Suddenly it hits him and he sits upright, with a bit more zeal and he smiles…maybe this is Fate sending him in a new direction. Maybe it's time for the swan to re-emerge as the ugly duckling once more, time for Adam Pope to return home for good and be content to live out the rest of his life in Lanesboro…regardless of what that life may be or how long. He does know that one way or another he'll have to atone for his sins whether it is as Zachariah or a re-born Adam and he's willing to accept the consequences whenever and however they may come. But then again, is it Fate or could this be the hand of God reaching out to him, redeeming him and putting him back on the same path his father so devotedly followed…maybe that's what this is, a calling! Is it time for him to be brought back into the fold and follow in his daddy's footsteps…time for Preacher Adam Pope to emerge from the cocoon that once was Zachariah Allmass? Zach doesn't understand why but tears are streaming down his cheeks, with this very sudden revelation and he quickly looks back to make sure Frank is still asleep and has not laid witness to this event and he wipes them away. "Hallelujah!" Zach shouts internally. "I'm going home!"

They arrive in Glenford late in the morning of the second day of their road trip and Frank's driving. They've made good time, less time than Frank thought considering the amount of unexpected road construction they encountered along the way. The Glenford bank is a brick foundation, one story building with a variety of stone features on its exterior walls which are divided into two bays on one side and another three on the other with a slate roof. The main entrance is on one corner in a recessed entryway with concrete steps to access it and features a rounded archway leading to the interior. It's a unique looking building and Frank can understand why they wanted to preserve it as he pulls up and parks.

"I won't be long." Zach says as he exits and goes in.

Frank takes the opportunity to get out, stretch his legs and get some fresh air by walking up the short block and back again before leaning against the hood waiting for Zach. Fifteen minutes later Zach comes out carrying a large cardboard banker box and places it on the back seat. Frank tosses him the keys. "You drive. I'll sit in the back so I can go through things. You know where you're going?"

Frank asks. Zach shakes his head at Frank's sarcastic question. He knows their expected route well. They're just eight hundred miles, about ten hours driving, south-east of Lanesboro now. A short distance compared to where they started this expedition from. They'll be taking the I-90 through Chicago and then on to their old home town of Lanesboro and Zach's getting excited about returning. Most of his childhood memories of there were…unpleasant, except for the summer he spent with Frank but maybe time does heal all wounds and wash away those recollections that were meant to stay in the past. For him, he knows it's time to leave things to Frank, the Handlers and the Tsiatko to sort out this crazy world. He's had his fill.

As soon as they are in motion, Frank flips off the lid of the banker box and starts going through it all. He's not sure what he's looking for, not sure what he'll find but his gut tells him something important is buried in here. He tries skimming through it first, hoping something will jump out at him. As he goes through the documentation, he notices Zach keeps checking on him in the rear view mirror. It's probably just curiosity. As time and the miles go by, Frank finds no revelations. They're now in Chicago, the halfway point to Lanesboro and Zach stops to fill up.

"Want anything?" Zach asks before he goes in to pay for the gas.

"Sure, how about a sandwich and a water." He replies.

"That's it?" Zach says.

Frank nods. Zach heads in and Frank exits to get some air again, leaning on the hood to survey the visible Chicago skyline. As he gazes, his mind drifts to Lanesboro, unsure of what he expects to find there. Will this be a wasted trip chasing something imagined?

Zach returns to see Frank staring off, unaware of his approach. "You okay?" He asks.

"Huh?" Frank says turning to him. "Yea…you okay with driving still?" Frank replies.

"No problem." Zach replies and they eat leaning against the SUV, saying nothing, each anxious in his own way, as they contemplate what may be coming next. They clamber in with Frank in the back seat again and they continue on his pilgrimage. Frank decides to go a different route with his search and instead inspects everything for anything that may purposely concealed, pages possibly stuck together or potential references written in the margins that may provide a lead. He's working the second journal of Mr. H's that he found in the castle and while examining the binding, he notices that the last page is not…the last page. The paper in those days was much heavier and the end sheet actually appears to be carefully glued down over the inside back cover. It's hard to discern visually but Frank can feel the outline of it with his finger tips, it's concealing something square in shape. He reaches over the seat and gets a knife from his duffle bag and carefully cuts near the outline of whatever appears to be in there. He uses the blade tip to pull up the unglued paper exposing a black and white photograph in remarkably good condition. He picks it up amazed to see it's of Ivan and Dasha flanked by a younger man and woman. "What the fuck?" He mutters wondering why his grandparents would be in a picture in Mr. H's journal.

Zach flashes him a look. "What is it? He asks.

Frank is concentrates on the images and doesn't hear Zach.

"Frank! What is that?!" Zach repeats.

Frank doesn't respond as a flash of a memories come flooding back, so strong he feels a twinge of pain in his temples. He knows the younger woman beside Dasha…it's is his adoptive mother Elena. He only vaguely recalls her but recognizes her more from the funeral card Dasha once showed him. He has no idea who the young guy in the picture beside Ivan is. Zach can easily read the look of surprise and shock on Frank's face in the rear view mirror.

"Frank! What is it?!" Zach shouts again, straining to keep his attention on the road.

Frank slides forward in his seat, and reaches over to hand Zach the picture. "Do you recognize the guy on the end beside Ivan?" He asks.

Zach tries to get a good look, still struggling to keep the wheel straight. "Where did you find a picture of Mr. H with your grandparents?" He says. "And who's the woman?"

"What do mean Mr. H?" Frank exclaims and clambers over the seat to get in the front. Frank grabs the wheel so Zach can have a closer look.

Zach keeps the pressure steady on the gas pedal while Frank steers. "Yea, that's Mr. H." Zach confirms. "I've seen enough pictures of him in the Committees archives to be sure." He takes the wheel back from Frank handing him the picture back. "Who's the woman?"

Frank slides over to the passenger side, staring down at her in the photograph. "I'm sure that's my adoptive mother." He says.

"Jesus Christ." Zach says. "Why are they all together?"

Frank shakes his head. "I have no idea." He flips the picture to check the back. There's a hand written notation, it's faded but easily legible, it reads — Family visit to the old country, sister Elena with Uncle Ivan and Aunt Dasha. "Fuck me." Frank says slowly extending it back to Zach.

Zach reads the back. "Holy shit, how is that possible?" Zach says looking equally perplexed as he returns it to Frank.

Frank silently takes it and leans back in the seat staring off at the passing views from his side window. There're in southeast Minnesota now and the area is teeming with woods and rivers but he's unaware of his surroundings as a million scenarios are playing out in his mind. He suddenly recalls an entry in Mr. H's journal from the castle; he drops the picture on the seat and reaches back for it. It's a bit of a hunt to find the reference he's looking for but he does. "This is an entry from the time Mr. H was interviewing candidates for Roswell." Frank says before reading from the journal. "I personally interview each candidate. I prefer them to be single and able to live on base with no close family ties to distract them. I myself have one sibling and a couple distant relatives, but I have not communicated with them for over a decade." Frank sets the journal down and picks up the picture. "His relatives," He says waving the picture. "Are, were his sister Elena and his aunt and uncle, Dasha and Ivan."

Zach doesn't know what to say, he's as shocked as Frank at this discovery. He had never uncovered any communications, notes or anything that suggested Mr. H had a family. However Mr. H hid their existence, he did it extremely well.

"Pull over somewhere." Frank instructs. "I need to…just pull in somewhere." It takes a few minutes but Zach finds a turn off, an overgrown trail that becomes a winding pathway into the dense woods of elder, maple, birch, elm, oak and pine. He stops about a mile in, once they're well camouflaged by the trees, Frank gets out and strolls about a hundred feet into the wilderness. Zach hits the remote, locking the SUV and trails not far behind him. Frank finds a fallen, gnarled, beaver chewed log and takes a seat, his perch reminds Zach of the one he and Frank shared on their many camping nights as kids and he can't help but smile about those days long past, briefly reminiscing of the fun they had that summer together. "They knew…son of a bitch, they all knew what I was…they had too." Frank mutters.

"Yea," Zach says hesitantly. "It does seem that way."

"It's hard to make sense of it." Frank adds. "Was it all a show? Ah, shit!" He doesn't know what to think. Frank sits quietly, struggling with it all and Zach lets him be. After a couple minutes Frank turns to Zach. "Like what the hell?!" He asks. Zach knows Franks is not looking for a response. Zach's role is simply to be a mute sounding board as Frank would have been having this same interaction with a tree or the piece of timber they're parked on had Zach not been present. "Was that why they gave me my independence at such an early age, gave me my space, the isolation I so craved, the rifle…all those endless sayings of Ivan's that he repeated over and over again? Were they really meant to empower and inspire me…to help prepare me?"

"Prepare you for what?" Zach asks quietly even though his words seem to echo out among the woods.

"For this, whatever the hell THIS is!" Frank replies. He gets up and walks out ten feet through the dense undergrowth and stands there reflecting on it all, an endless array of questions that he knows he'll never have answers to, run through his head. He finally turns to Zach. "Was that everything in that box? You're not holding anything back are you?"

"I swear Frank, that's all there is."

"I just don't need any more surprises." Frank says. His eyes are cold but not black.

"That's all I've got, seriously."

Frank turns his back to Zach again.

After a moment Zach speaks up. "Look, this may not be the time and I don't know how much this may screw up whatever plans you have but when we get done whatever we're doing in Lanesboro, I'm not going any further with you. I've decided I'm going to stay there. I'm done with everything, the Committee, the Handlers…you. Things are too screwed up and I've decided I'm going to try and make a fresh start there…as Adam Pope. It's time for me to be where I think I really belong." He says.

Frank looks back. "Why are you telling me this?"

Zach stands. "As much as I hate to admit this, I'm telling you this because you're the closest thing I have to a friend in this world." Even though Frank's back is to him, Zach can see Frank shaking his head at Zach's confession.

Frank turns to Zach, drawing his silencer equipped Glock from his shoulder holster as he does.

Mr. H's warning means more to him now than ever before…trust no one.

"What the fuck Frank?!" Zach exclaims.

Frank calmly fires, the shot penetrates Zach's forehead, explodes out the back of his head and the slug is lost in the thick of the forest, it will never be found. He wanted some distance between himself and Zach, to avoid any blowback from the blood spatter. He wasn't expecting Zach to share, not that it would matter what he had to say…the outcome would have been the same. Zach back flips over the log from the impact, dead and Frank strolls over and puts two more in his lifeless chest. He places a foot on the log, resting his forearms on his now elevated knee to view the lifeless corpse before him. Frank examines Zach's death mask, his face is frozen in an expression of shock and surprise. For Frank, this is simply the way it has to be…he doesn't need to justify his actions, he simply takes action. "This was a long time coming Zach, you never should have sent that team after me in Belize. I don't forgive or forget…and regardless of you believing that you saved my life back in the castle and no matter how much you revealed to me about myself, in the end, you knew too much and… I just can't have that." Frank confesses to his dead comrade. He steps over the disfigured bole that was Zach's seat and carefully rifles through his pockets, taking the fob and key, his cash and anything else he can find, surprisingly Zach isn't armed. Frank backtracks, searching through the ground growth for his expended brass which he finds and pockets. He tosses a few pine boughs that are scattered about, over the corpse and on his way to the SUV, he scans back to see if anything is clearly visible that Zach was violently laid to rest there. It's going to a long time before anybody discovers he's there, by then the wildlife will have devoured most of the remains, they'll be nothing left but bones, just like Mr. H.

Frank climbs into the driver's seat, smiles and breathes a sigh of a relief at how good it feels to finally have Zach out of the way; he was too much of a distraction…Frank knew full well he just needed to be patient and wait for the right time and place. Frank examines his now cherished photo once more before tucking it away in his shirt pocket, picks up Mr. H's journal off the front seat, tosses it in the back and heads toward the highway; next stop, Lanesboro.

CHAPTER ELEVEN

Frank's trying to concentrate on the road but his mind is still trying to process all he's just learned about his grandparents, his second mom and Mr. H…all being related. They knew what he was and kept the secret, never revealing it to him. Well, they did tell him, after the fact….the fact being, they were dead when they did it in and accomplished it in their own lunatic way and what a crazy way it was. He wants to be mad at them for leaving him in the dark for so long but he knows he never would've believed their lunatic story when he was younger…hell, he had a hard time accepting it when it came from Zach with all his evidence and later confirmed by Willow. Shit, as he glances back at the carton of papers, he's still having problems with it. And if he would've believed them, would things have turned out any different, would he have chosen a different path or, in truth, would the bread crumbs placed for him to follow been different? He doubts it. What is this Power that he so firmly believes in that has led him down these paths he has followed all his life on this world? Is it actually the Orb…its very presence on this world being his guiding light? The influence of the previous occupations, the Handlers…Fate or all of them combined? Whatever it is, it's strong. "Fuck." He mumbles and pulls over to the shoulder. He's suddenly realized he phased out with his thoughts and is disoriented now as to how far he's been driving while under the influence of his musings and where he actually is. "Concentrate." He orders to no one other than himself as he pulls back on the road, accelerating hard to get ahead of the flow of vehicles coming up from behind.

He anxiously drives about ten miles before a sign comes up that gives him a lead as to where he is and he feels less tense, Christ he hates it when he does that! He keeps himself fixated on his driving and an hour later, he's approaching

Lanesboro which is nestled in the Root River Valley, a scenic countryside of hills and bluffs. He doesn't recognize anything on the outskirts but surmises a few decades of absence will do this. Things were on the dire side when he left but obviously the economics have changed with the amount of advertising and billboards he sees as he nears, promoting an array of historical and cultural attractions including Amish tours, theatres, restaurants, inns and motels, recreational tours, museums; the list goes on. His old homestead is on the other side of town and he was hoping to avoid going through Lanesboro but he's too unfamiliar with things now and has no choice. His burner phones have no data so he's left navigating old school and he trusts they have a tourist information site so he can grab a map and re-orientate to these old surroundings.

He spots a sign promoting a Visitor's Centre and follows the arrows and additional signage along the way, leading him to Railway Avenue which was and still is the main drag. A lot has changed but hasn't. He's impressed that most of the old buildings he remembers are still standing but have been painstakingly restored; the place still has that old, small town feel. Where the obvious transformation has taken place is in its thriving revitalization from tourism. When he left, the Lanesboro was dying, today the main street is now a bustle of people and every space is occupied with the many enterprises advertised on the way in. It's once again a busy little centre as it once was. Frank has no time for sight-seeing though, he's on a mission and locates the Visitor's Centre on the North end of Railway. He's just one among the bustle of people as he enters and begins to browse through the various complimentary maps and brochures on one of the stands.

"Frank Smirnov…my God, is that really you?" A woman's voice calls out.

Frank ignores the voice and continues flipping through the information rack. "C'mon, c'mon, where the hell is a town map?" He mutters. Out of the corner of his eye, he watches as an elderly woman standing behind the service counter, nimbly comes around and approaches him. "Christ!" He whispers. He tries to turn away but the woman gently puts a hand on his arm.

"You're Frank Smirnov, aren't you?" She asks.

Frank turns to her and looks into her crystal clear blue eyes. She's a small, frail, white haired, elderly woman with a slight stoop to her and he estimates she has to be in her nineties. He has no idea who she is or how she could possibly recognize him.

"Oh!" She exclaims, smiling and placing her hands to her cheeks, "I'd recognize those eyes anywhere. I thought you must have been dead, you've been gone so long!"

"I'm sorry," Frank says. "Are you sure you don't have me confused with someone else?"

She laughs. "Still trying to keep in your own little world I see."

Frank involuntarily grins.

"I knew it." She says, lightly slapping her thigh.

Frank shakes his head slightly in amazement, he's been caught. "You have me at a disadvantage." He says chuckling.

Her face is beaming. "I'm Lydia Hemshaw; I was one of your teachers in high school." She announces.

"Hemshaw?" Frank ponders the name for a moment. "Sorry, it's not ringing any bells." He says.

"Blast it." She replies, "Been using that name for so long…that's my married name. It was Warwick back then."

Frank immediately recognizes the name but can't put the younger Warwick's face to it. "I do remember you." He admits nodding but is not willing to take the conversation any further.

Lydia recognizes this immediately. "You haven't changed a bit," She says. "Still the turtle in the shell. Okay, I'll let you off the hook." She giggles. "What brings you back?"

Frank silently thanks her for recognizing this. "I found myself in the area and thought I'd swing by the old homestead and possibly the cemetery but it's been so long, nothing looks familiar so I'm looking for a local map." He says.

"Hang on." And she goes to the counter and grabs a map from a display. "Here," She says, handing it to him. "This will lead you where you need to go but I have to warn you, there's not much left standing at your old place."

"Thank you. Do you mind refreshing my memory on the map where the cemetery is? I know it's out of town a ways." He asks.

"Of course," She replies unfolding the map on the counter. "You follow this road here and it will take you to the old church site which is about here," Pointing to a spot several miles out of town. "But watch, if you find yourself on this bridge you've gone too far. The place is pretty over grown and tough to see from the road."

"No one uses it anymore?" He asks.

She comes up close. "That place has been shut down for close to thirty-five years now." She whispers. "Not that I was ever out there myself but talk was the place was haunted…me, I think those folks were probably a cult or something to have such crazy notions, sampling potions and all that kind of stuff to say they saw all they say they did. Mark my word, hallucinatinations from whatever they were drinking or smoking."

Frank is a bit taken aback by your comments but at the same time, it leaves him wondering if something else was at play. "Okay, I'll take that into account if I head out there. Thanks and how about we don't share you bumping into me." He whispers back.

"You never change. Mums the word. Take care of yourself and it was good seeing you whether you liked it or not." She mutters smiling.

Frank nods his appreciation and leaves without looking back. Once in his vehicle he takes a minute to review the directions again before he heads home, just a mile away, not sure what to expect when he gets there. He's reminded of Ivan's words, "We'll be waiting for you." Will he find apparitions of his grandparents lingering there for him? As he nears the old place, the landscape has changed so much over the years, nothing is recognizable and he finds he has passed what was once a location he was so familiar with. He turns around and slows down as he tries to find that long laneway leading to the old farm. "Impossible." He mutters as he pulls into an approach. Lydia was right, not much is left standing, nothing actually. His gaze is drawn to a small hillside as he clambers out, the place where once sat a small two story house and a variety of outer buildings. There's nothing left, no remnants of what once was, only a small grassy knoll and trees. Even the well traveled laneway is all but gone, its edges now barely discernible. He walks to the four strand barb wire fence cutting him off from the property, leans against a post and watches for some kind of sign…something to justify this odyssey.

"Is everything alright?" A male voice calls out to Frank.

Frank looks back to see a police cruiser parked on the highway just behind his SUV, the roof top light bar is lit up and the passenger window down. A smiling deputy is looking at him. Frank turns to face him, pulling his coat closed so that his shoulder holster stays concealed. "Hi, all good, just taking a break and checking out the scenery. Am I trespassing?" He asks as he takes a couple steps toward the car.

"No," The Deputy laughs. "Just making sure everything is okay. We're a small community and we like to make sure everyone is looked after."

"You don't hear that too often anymore." Frank says faking a smile hoping the Deputy doesn't decide to give his vehicle an inspection. He doesn't want to have to put him down, he looks pretty young.

"Unfortunately you're right there. Well, you have a good day and hopefully you'll enjoy your stay." He replies.

"Actually, just passing through." Frank says.

"Well, enjoy your passing through." The Deputy says chuckling, gives Frank a salute, shuts off his bar lights and moves on.

Frank gets behind the wheel of the SUV and continues to watch the yard space that's been abandoned to nature. What now? The cemetery? That would make more sense, not that there is anything sensible about any of this. That's where they'll physically be waiting…six feet down but none the less. He shakes his head. "What the fuck am I doing here?" He asks himself as he re-checks the map. Wisel Cemetery is ten miles south of Lanesboro which means a drive back through town. He hates exposing his presence here, and not for any logical reason but, a cop has already seen him and Lydia has recognized him so what difference is it going to make. He gets to the south end of Lanesboro, turns onto highway twenty-one and watches for the turn off onto to twelve which will take him where he needs to go. The church is just off of twelve, right by a dense small forest, a couple hundred yards from the South Fork Root River. He rounds a bend that takes him to a small bridge over the river. "Shit!" He exclaims knowing now, he's gone too far. He finds a spot to turn around and slows down as he makes his way back around the bend. He finds the turnoff into the church yard; it definitely appears to have been abandoned a long time ago. The SUV pushes through the hanging branches at the lane entrance and enters a small clearing. The decrepit old church with its badly flaking white wash paint job is still standing but has been boarded up a long time ago. The front steps are busted apart, the walls are battered, there're visible holes in the roof and what once was the steeple, is lying shattered on the ground. Parked near it is a rusted quarter-ton truck and a grizzled old man is loading an old push mower into the box, using boards for ramps. Frank pulls up and gets out. "Good day." He says and extends his hand for a shake as he moves toward him.

The old guy has a grip like a vice; his hands are large and calloused. Close up, Old Guy looks like he's a hundred. His face is full of deep wrinkles that are accentuated by his dark tan which makes his face look like etched leather. He has a patchy, snow white bristle for a beard and the hair that is peeking out from his full brim, sweat stained and frayed straw hat is bright white as well. He seems short but his back is so stooped it's hard to tell. He's wearing a dirty white, long sleeved shirt and faded, torn bib coveralls with heavily scuffed brown leather work boots that have seen better days. He pulls a soiled red checked cloth handkerchief from his back pocket and wipes his face. "You lost boy?" He asks.

Frank laughs at his bluntness. "I've been feeling that way for quite some time now." He admits.

"You must be, ain't no other reason why anyone would be here otherwise." Old Guy says. His tired looking physical appearance may suggest the years but his bright green eyes still hint that he has a lot more life left in him.

Frank looks around. "You look after the place?" He asks

"It's not by choice that I'm out here." Old Guy says and Frank's question seems to sink in after the fact. "And ... what the hell boy; does this place look like its look after? You lost AND blind?" Old Guy adds.

Frank can't help but laugh at Old Guy's sarcastic wit. "I came out here to check out the graveyard."

"Why?" He asks.

"I like old graveyards." Frank replies.

"You sure you don't have some other reason for being here?" Old Guy asks. He suddenly seems a bit anxious.

"Why would I?" Frank answers suspiciously as Old Guy's question seems odd. "I'm just a guy looking for a cemetery.

"Aw, Christ....son of a bitch, I'm never gonna get away from this place." Old Guy mutters, waving the hand still clutching the handkerchief in the direction of the graveyard as he turns away. Here takes a couple shuffled steps toward his truck before facing Frank again. "I thought you was here because all those strange going ons that happened. It's been a long time but you never know. Over thirty years ago since they buried anyone here and I don't know how many years since anyone's stopped by." Old Guy says taking a seat on the rear bumper of his truck. "That's why I thought you was here for? I mean, why else would anyone come out here anymore?"

"What do you mean?"

Although they're in the middle of nowhere, Old Guy looks around like he's scared of being overheard. "I ain't supposed to talk about but I use to be the gravedigger here and, well…we had some spooky stuff happening way back. Nothing that could be explained." He says.

"Like what?" Frank asks. This may be where he's supposed to be after all.

"It'll be easier if I show you what started all the ruckus." He stands and points to the church. "And the church damage there? That didn't happen on its own." He says as he hobbles past the decaying building in the direction that Frank knows, is to the cemetery. "But I ain't going in." He adds.

"Going in where, the church?" Franks asks.

"The graveyard, dam nit…don't tell me you have trouble hearing too!"

Frank chuckles and comes up along aside Old Guy and they make their way to the graveyard which is a few hundred feet away from the church. Old Guy pulls a flask from his back pocket, takes a hearty swig of what smells like whiskey and passes it to Frank.

"No thanks." Frank says.

"You sure, you might need it?"

"I'm sure." Frank says smiling.

Old Guy takes another guzzle before capping it and tucking it away. Once they exit the church yard, they are also past a small protective border of trees and the graveyard comes into view. They are knee deep in a field of grass and alfalfa as they tromp onward. Two hundred feet later, they stop at what once was a gated entrance to the burial ground which is bordered on two sides by heavy woods. It's once solid and straight chicken wire fence is in disarray, posts rotted away and most if it lying on the ground, covered in vine; almost all of the grave markers are invisible, hidden from view by tall weeds and quack grass. This graveyard has not seem any loving care for ages and based on Old Guy's demeanor as they had neared, probably from fear of intruding on what does not want to be disturbed.

Old Guy takes one more drink and points to the far corner of the cemetery, coincidentally, the location where Frank's grandparents had been laid to rest.

It's hard for Frank to discern where the trees end and the cemetery begins as he looks in the direction of Ivan and Dasha's final resting place. Frank walks across the fallen rusted metal gate now entwined with the ground vegetation and makes his way to their graves. "You coming?" Frank asks, looking back at Old Guy as he walks.

Old Guy hesitates. "Lord, help me." He says crossing himself as he enters.

Frank passes the remains of a half dug grave along the way, barely discernible by the overgrowth. A long handled steel spade, its wood shaft rotted, is still planted in the overgrown mound of dirt that once was one with the cavity. Old Guy, a few feet behind, pauses at the hole. He quickly scans the graveyard before scampering on to catch up to Frank, nearly walking into him as Frank halts twenty feet from his grandparents' markers. "Unbelievable." Frank says as moves closer to inspect their grave site. Their stone markers are hardly worn, seemingly totally unaffected by the weather since the day they were installed and fresh flowers are lying at their bases. There's an imaginary rectangular border extending four feet out in all directions from their plots where the grass appears to be freshly cut, whereas every other grave is covered in thick tall foliage. What gives this sight a sinister edge is that the plots are bordered on all sides by evenly spaced large trees implanted upside down with their expansive bare roots extending a dozen feet in the air, forming a canopy over the graves, as if to offer further protection from the elements; Frank knows what these are, they're called Bigfoot Markers, in this case Tsiatko, and it's a warning to keep out.

Frank turns to Old Guy. "How long ago did this happen?"

"Like I told you boy, over thirty years and this was no one time deal. Now can we get out of here and talk back at the church?"

"And just these two graves?" Frank asks.

"Damn it boy!" Old Guy exclaims. "Look around! You see this anywhere else?! I'm outta here! I'm way too old for this shit!"

Frank grabs Old Guy by his overall strap and flips back his own coat to reveal his holstered automatic. "You're going nowhere until I hear it all." He warns him.

"I guess you ain't here outta curiosity after all, are you?"

"Good guess." Frank answers.

Old Guy looks deep in Frank's eyes, he's the one, has to be…Old Guy is praying silently he is. He shakes himself loose from Frank's grip. "It didn't start til maybe a year after they were buried." Meaning Frank's grandparents. "The up-turned trees, that's what stated it all off. I was taken care of everything back then, diggin graves too. At first there were only a couple and when we pulled them out, they were eight, ten feet in the ground. No tire marks, no tracks from equipment, nothing to show the holes were dug first either. But as soon as we yanked them out, a couple days later they were replaced, in new spots. So we kept pulling them out and not by hand, had to use a damn tractor with a bucket and chain to do it… but in no time, new ones would be back. It went on for weeks and as time went on, two became three and then more and more until the graves were surrounded, just like you see them now. We gave up and thought that would be the end of it all but strange things starting happening at the church next. During mass, rocks thrown against the church, pounding on the walls, loud strange whooping and hollering…inhuman sounds that no one ever heard before. The minister made everyone take a vow not to talk about it outside the congregation." Old Guy says, stopping to look at the nearby tree-line. "Look mister, it's gonna be night soon, can we talk elsewhere, I don't wanna be here when it's dark." He pleads.

"Just talk."

Old Guy starts bouncing a bit, he's getting antsy. "Something wanted everyone out of here permanently and things got worse. Invisible Hellions starting ripping away at the church walls and roof and when we put armed men out, it just hap-pened in the dead of night instead. In the middle of all this going on, some white haired preacher from Lanesboro showed up proclaiming how all this was our own fault. That we brought this upon us because we buried those who raised a demon in our consecrated ground. I don't know if you knew those folks buried in them two spots and no disrespect, but he was referrin to those two graves there." Old Guy says pointing to Ivan and Dasha's markers. "Many followers quit coming cause they were too scared."

Frank knows who that white haired preacher had to be…Zachariah's daddy.

"Some of the congregation, the few that stuck around, was starting to believe that white haired preacher, even though most thought he was a bit crazy. One night that preacher led a bunch of the church goers here to dig up the graves so they could take the remains down by the river, burn them and scatter the ashes in the water."

"What?!" Frank asks.

"Based on your concern, I'd say you knew those folks buried there, but don't fret, it never happened. Those that went with him were never seen again. Only the preacher was left, come morning, pacing in the front of the church which was pretty much wrecked like you see it now. All he kept rambling about was how large demons that reeked of hell itself took the souls of those with him, took their souls and placed them into the very trees that surrounded these graves. That he was left standing only because he knew the truth, that he was the righteous one…me, I think the guy was a nut job." Old Guy cups his hands to his mouth. "Alright…I dun what I was supposed to do…please…let me get on with my life?" Old Guy shouts out begging.

Frank checks the woods, wondering who the hell Old Guy is yelling to. "What do you mean you've done what you're supposed to do?" Frank asks.

Old Guy removes his hat, rolling the brim in his hands and places it against his chest. "You think I've been coming here every day for the last thirty some years, cutting grass just to pass the time? Cause I want to? I…I never told anyone this but…I was here the night those men went missing. I had no part in what they were trying to do…I was working, digging that grave we passed yonder. I saw it all boy…I saw it all." Old Guy is reliving the experience and he shutters as a chill runs up his spine. "No sir, I've been waiting for a man like you, searching for this place so I could tell what happened. That's what I was ordered that night, after the ones who dunnit let me be. And at the end of my story, I'm supposed to tell you that knowin and understandin ain't the same thing but they're entwined." Old Guy looks up at the heavens before looking back at Frank. "Wasn't sure I was gonna live long enough to see this through."

Frank takes a step toward Old Guy. "What, who told you to tell me that?! Was it an older man dressed kind of like you?!" Frank demands.

Old Guy shakes his head. "Was no man that told me…was nuthin human at all."

"Who…what then?!" Frank asks loudly.

"Sweet Jesus." Old Guy blurts out crossing himself. His face has gone death white, even with his tanned complexion…he turns and runs like the devil himself is chasing him.

Frank spins around to witness Brother and a half dozen Tsiatko emerging from the woods. They circumvent the markers and Brother stops to face Frank, the other Tsiatko flank him. Frank bows his head and closes his eyes. He takes a deep breath and shakes his head…their message is hitting home; they're all in on it. He's still the puppet on a string, being played by others. He looks up at Brother wondering if this is their way of showing him who's really in control.

"The Orb is at risk but we will ensure it does not fall into the hands of those that have no right to it…it will be back in your possession soon." Brother says.

"What do you mean at risk? Are the Handlers in danger?" Frank asks.

Brother approaches and lightly places his massive hand on Frank's shoulder. "Do not worry my brethren,it is as it's supposed to be. You must learn to stop questioning and accept the path you have been given to follow."

Frank dislodges Brother's hand in frustration. "You know, I'm really getting sick of these bullshit answers." Frank replies.

"It is time for you to go." Brother states.

"Go where?" Frank asks.

"The next stage, you should understand what is expected of you by now." Brother states.

Motherfuckers, they all think they know him, the Tsiatko, the Handlers, his grandparents; Christ…even Mr. H has been playing him. "Expected of me?" Frank replies sarcastically, not caring whether his tone is understood or not.

"Yes." Brother replies. "It is time for redemption…for all, in their own way."

CHAPTER TWELVE

"Where did you obtain this video?" A Committee Member asks.

"From our informant." The Male Voice Committee Member answers. "The one we have inside the little group Ms. Byrnes has assembled."

"And how long have you had this before you decided to share it with the rest of us?" Another Member demands.

"I did nothing inappropriate. I only took the time to ensure its authenticity. In this day and age it's easy to be…creative." The Male Voice answers.

"And?" Another one of the video displayed Members asks.

"It's legitimate." The Male Voice replies.

"How was this person able to get such footage? It appears to be taken from a higher elevation. Is this from a drone?" A Member asks.

"It is. What better candidate to watch over things than the very same person who's watching over things." The Male Voice answers. The others can hear the smugness in its voice.

"Enough with the riddles. Explain." A Member says.

"Robert Montgomery." The Male Voice announces.

"Who's that suppose to be?" Another Member asks.

"Mr. Robert Montgomery was the head of the drone units assigned to Belette's teams during their hunts for the Tsiatko, modern technology at work although we knew it would be of little value for tracking the Tsiatko." The Male Voice answers.

"Who is we?" A Member barks. "Get to the point. I do not have the time or the patience for your games or your gloating."

"Let me have a little enjoyment from this game of chess Ms. Byrnes has elected to play with us. Us, being the Committee the same as we being the Committee." The Male Voice answers.

"You may say we but obviously you have been either making decisions on behalf of the Committee or withholding crucial information from us…the Committee, neither of which is acceptable. You can face the same consequences as any that cross us…you appear to be overstepping your bounds." A Member warns.

"I humbly apologize if it seems so." The Male Voice says sincerely. "I have not withheld or taken any action that was against our protocols. I had simply put safeguards into place to monitor the activity of the teams, specifically Allmass who was leading them at the time. I had suspicions that he had placed his personal priorities above those of the Committee and I was looking for proof of that before I brought it before this judicious council. I took advantage of Ms. Byrnes offer to Montgomery when he informed me of her request, to have Montgomery clandestinely monitor her and her group's activities. It was not until I received this video that I had any substantial evidence and that is why we are gathered today."

"Continue." A Member says.

"To provide you all with some back history, the teams assigned to hunting the Tsiatko believed they were working for some unnamed corporation but Mr. Montgomery was specifically recruited by me, on behalf of the Committee and he was fully aware of that fact. Yes, his assigned task was to do reconnaissance for the teams but his real agenda was monitoring what directives Allmass was giving them with the priority to surveil Allmass at every opportunity."

"And what came of this?" A Member asks.

"Nothing. Everything seemed to as it appeared and so I had nothing to disclose to the Committee. I took this secondary placement of Montgomery solely based on my…intuition." The Male Voice says. "It was not a decision that required Committee approval." The Male Voice's response is met with silence from the other Members. "To me something was not right about Ms. Byrnes but I respected the Committee's decision to have her replace Belette." The Male Voice adds, breaking the quiet.

"Why did you not bring up your concerns?" A Member inquires.

"Because the guiding principle of the Committee is that we only deal with fact. Not conjecture, not gut feelings, not suspicions…fact." The Male Voice answers.

"You are correct. Please proceed with what evidence you presume you now have." Another Member states.

"The AR is a key position within our operation and, within specific guidelines, has the authority to speak and act on the Committee's behalf. For me, Ms. Byrnes was coming up the ladder too quickly. She's a reputable psychologist and I believe she had Belette under her spell, knew exactly how to play him. Do I need remind everyone that soon after Belette initially brought her on board, his Head of Security suddenly died and it was her candidate that took the position?"

"Cut to the chase." A Member interrupts.

The Male Voice plays the video freezing it on the frame clearly displaying Allmass and Smirnov talking on the grounds that Montgomery had taped, for all the Members to see. "This is my evidence. Why is this hybrid rebel that she reported dead with DNA evidence for proof, freely walking the grounds her and her entourage are occupying, conversing with Allmass who supposedly was undercover to stem the rebellion that this very crossbreed was leading?" The Male Voice exclaims. "Why? Because there was no undercover operation with Allmass, there was no rebellion, Ms. Byrnes and her comrades slaughtered everyone to make it appear they were staving off a rebellion so they could infiltrate our operation and start a mutiny with the aid of Allmass, Smirnov and probably every damn Tsiatko on this planet in hopes of destroying us! The very thing we feared most! And she may have gotten away with it if it were not for MY intuitions!" The Male Voice says, having accentuated this more as a means of self redemption than anything else. "And if she's lied about Smirnov's death, leaving him to live a life of freedom under our very noses, you can be assured the Orb is not in the hands of the Tsiatko as she stated either." The Male Voice takes a moment to change the image on the screen, now displaying the still from the cavern showing the Orb in between Allmass and Smirnov with the obvious forms of the Tsiatko in the background. "These two would not have left the Orb behind. If they're at our Klamath location, so is the Orb. They're probably hiding out in the bunker; the same place the supposed rebellion took place which would make sense as there's no video surveillance there."

There's silence once more from the Members and one finally breaks the silence. "Obviously you must already have a suggested course of action?"

"I do. We use full size military drones mounted with hellfire torpedoes to level the mansion and guest house and follow that with a large scale assault team to clean everything up and recover the Orb. If anyone survives the air strike, the ground assault teams will take them out, if any take refuge in the bunker, they've got no place to go and the assault teams will deal with them accordingly. We end this once and for all." The Male Voice answers.

"This seems to echo the opinions of those who charged the cavern at Mt. Rainier. That outcome was not favorable to our cause." A Member states. "If we take this action, are you prepared to put your life on the line and pay the same price as Belette did for his failures?"

"I am. We are advancing against human traitors. We're not attacking the Tsiatko on their home turf. There are no Tsiatko at Klamath, of this I am positive." The Male Voice replies.

"Are you sure you're not being naïve about that statement?" A Member asks.

"I am certain." The Male Voice replies.

"And if we sanction this…what about the local authorities and news agencies?" A Member asks concerned.

"Excuse my language but, fuck them. It's an isolated location with a single road access from the two adjoining highways so we'll set up manned construction detour signs at each end. As far as air traffic, there's none, corporate or private, that's one of the reasons we chose Klamath in the first place, isolation. So we won't put out a no-fly zone as that will only cause red flags. By the time anyone gets wind of it, if they do, we'll have the place leveled and secured." The Male Voice says.

"When?" A Member asks.

"Dawn tomorrow, we can't afford to wait. Do I have your consensus?" The Male Voice asks. The electronic voting completes and the endorsement is unanimous.

CHAPTER TWELVE

Its five-fifteen a.m. and Richard Montgomery hurriedly wakes his men from their sleep. "Get up…get up, if you want to live!" He loudly sings. "Better do as I say…the fires of perdition are coming boys and you don't want to be here when they do!"

"What's going on?" One of them groggily asks.

"There's no time for explanation! Just grab your clothes and get to the Humvee cause I'm leaving and whoever's not in, gets left behind to burn!" He exclaims smiling. "Yes!" He yells as he rambles about the room. "Yes! The keys… where are the keys? Oh," He chuckles. "They're right here in my hand." He looks back at his men. "It's show time." And he heads for the door. He's been waiting as long as he can before breaking out of the grounds, escaping the clutches of Ms. Byrnes and doesn't want to give the residents in the big house any advance notice of what's coming their way. He revs the engine and his men jump in, one of the back doors still ajar as he throws it in gear. He doesn't follow the lane but goes cross country across the grounds, plowing through hedges and tearing up the manicured lawn along the way, laughing with pure delight as he crashes through the gates of the Klamath grounds. He may believe his actions are quite sane but to his men, as all of them are being tossed about in the seats behind him, he's acting like a lunatic…a man deranged.

There's a loud knock on Willow's bedroom door and Stogie enters without waiting for a reply. She sits up. "What is it?" She asks.

"We have a problem." He says chomping down on his trademark unlit organic cigar before removing it, holding it between his index and middle fingers as he crosses his arm across his burly chest. "Montgomery and his crew just tore across the grounds and busted out through the front gates." He states calmly.

Willow flips back the covers and swings out of bed. "Okay, get everybody up and we'll meet in the kitchen. Tell them what happened and that they've got ten minutes to be there."

"This means something heavy is coming our way and probably pretty damn soon." Stogie adds.

"I know. We have time. I have to run to the bunker first, I'll be right back." She says and Stogie leaves. She had such high hopes that this time was going to be different but they're not done yet.

"That cow!" Montgomery shouts pounding on the steering wheel as he careens along the highway, the engine floored. "That fucking cow is going to pay!" Giggling now like someone unhinged. His men hang on for dear life, still unsure what to make if his actions and none daring to ask. "C'mon, c'mon, where is it? I know its close." He says no one in particular as he strains to see through the veil of darkness as the sun is not yet up. He weaves along the road hoping the headlights will light up the approach he's looking for. "There it is!" He shouts, slamming on the brake nearly unseating his men and turns sharply onto an old logging road. He has no choice but to slow as they begin a steep winding incline. "We're going to have the best view!" He shouts back to his men. They look at each other, unsure if they should appreciate that announcement or dread it and Montgomery begins to whistle some nameless tune as he drives. Twenty minutes later and after much jostling around, Montgomery comes to a halt between the thick trees on the crest of a hill overlooking the mansion grounds, its perimeter lights still visible in the dark of the early morn even though they're close to a mile away. He shuts off the headlights but leaves the motor running, reaches into a case of beer strapped into the passenger seat and cracks a cold one. He takes a gulp. "You boys want one?" He says as he looks in the rearview mirror and hands three back before they can answer. "This is going to be sweet! Men, you have the best... well, second best seat in the house for the fireworks and they are going to start," As he checks his watch. "In about ten minutes!" They hear them before they see them and Montgomery jumps out, followed by his team to view that recognizable sound of helicopters. They clamber down the slope about fifty to clear the trees so they have a better view skyward. Half a dozen Chinook transport helicopters are now hovering above them in a line matching the curved topography of the hill. Montgomery knows they're filled with members of the planned assault team, two hundred and sixty-four men in total.

"Whoohoo!" Montgomery yells upward, raising his beer to the sky but he's invisible to those waiting above. He guzzles it down, tossing the empty down the hill side and gets on all fours to climb back to the vehicle to grab another. He quickly slides back down on his rump, the beer case safely tucked away under his arm.

"What's going on boss?" One of his men asks.

"Watch…watch, they're coming!" Montgomery shouts and as those words escapes his lips, a dozen MQ-9 Reaper UAVs; unmanned air vehicles, their rear single prop engines barely discernible, pass over head, visible only because the sun has begun to rise.

Each Reaper is armed with two Hellfire missiles plus two GBU-12 Paveway bombs. They had been launched from Beale Air Force Base just south of them, ten miles north of Sacramento. The same location the Chinook Helicopters departed from. The drones form a V-formation and each one fires a Paveway laser controlled bomb, some at the guest house but most targeting the mansion. These projectiles are extremely precise and the thrust of their solid-fuel rocket motors are clearly evident as they accelerate to eight hundred miles per hour before they hit their targets. The flashes are brilliant as they hit home, the guest house and mansion are devastated. The drones circle around, each firing another Paveway, completely flattening what is left of the structures and the remnants of the mansion crumbles into the cavity that once was its basement. The Reapers pass once more and now fire all their Hellfire missiles, twenty-four in total which can penetrate any type of armor, each one has kill radius of sixty-five feet. If anything had survived the initial Paveways, nothing will outlive the Hellfires. The destruction is so decisive, there's nothing even left to burn, only small whiffs of smoke emanate from the ruins.

Bottle still in hand, Montgomery clasps both hands to his head as he looks on in amazement. "Holy fuck, holy fuck…holy fuck! Do you guys see that?! That was incredible?!" He screams.

His men don't know how to answer as they haven't a clue as to why all this just happened. They're just glad they were out of there in time. The Reapers disappear from sight and the Chinook helicopters move in. They land just inside the gates of the mansion grounds, a bevy of men disembark and the Chinooks lift off. A third of the assault team head to the remains of the structures while the remaining make a beeline for the bunker which is hidden from view among the fir trees on the west side of the property.

Montgomery lobs his empty and makes a mad scramble for the Humvee. "We gotta get down there…there's no way I'm missing this!" His men quickly follow and they load up. Montgomery throws it in reverse but travels no more than thirty feet before the vehicle is brought to an abrupt halt. He guns the engine and can hear the wheels spinning but the Humvee isn't budging. "Jesus, what now?" He says as he reaches for the door handle. Suddenly, the face of a Tsiatko fills his window. "Fuck!" He screams as its immense hand comes crashing through the auto-glass, grabbing him by the throat and crushing it with a single squeeze, nearly decapitating it from his body. The men in the rear watch in horror and try to exit through the rear doors but they're immediately slammed shut as soon as they try, closed with such force, it crumples the panels…there's no escape. In actuality, the vehicle is surrounded by Tsiatko who easily flip the Humvee on its roof and six of the gigantic Beings leap onto the undercarriage and begin jumping and stomping on the upturned vehicle. The military grade cabin and frame is no match against the six tons of force that's hammering down on it like a monstrous pile driver. The screams of Montgomery's men trapped inside fall on deaf ears and the Humvee is flattened into a fifteen inch high slab of metal in minutes. Streams of blood mixed with pulps of body parts, oil and fuel flow from the metal remains, spilling onto the ground. The avenging Tsiatko leap off the mass of steel to avoid the organic and petroleum ooze now spreading freely and join the rest of their ranks as they make their way down to the mansion grounds. They're frothing for redemption and nothing's going to stop them from having it.

CHAPTER THIRTEEN

The members of Team One are assigned the task of sifting through the mansion rubble looking for evidence that the targets have been taken out, their bosses want physical proof and they want to see remains…body parts, teeth, anything and everything. There's supposed to be six, possibly eight subjects in all. If they find no evidence in this initial search then heavy equipment will be brought in. Team Two is searching the remains of the guest house while the largest of the force, Team Three, is converging on the bunker. As Team One works away at their painstaking task, they're encountering hot spots among the destruction and solid footing is difficult among all the rubble but after thirty minutes of fruitless hunting, nothing is discovered to confirm the kills.

"Did you think it was going to be that easy?" A haunting female voice whispers through the headset of a Team One member. He whirls with his weapon at the ready and the only persons in his vision are those of his fellow team.

"What the fuck is wrong with you?!" The female confederate immediately behind him shouts.

"Did you hear that?" He asks.

"Hear what?!" She yells. "All I know is that your pointing a loaded weapon at me and you look like you're about to shit your pants! Get your act together!"

He shakes his head. "Yea, sorry…just, nothing…never mind." And he turns away.

"Get a grip before you shoot somebody!" She shouts back at him.

The haunting female voice giggles. "Can't you see us? We're right here." The Haunting Voice says through the headset, which now is being transmitted to all of Team One. They all turn, in almost perfect synchronization, hunting for its unknown source.

"Who's being the smart ass?! This is no time or place for fucking games!" The Team One Leader barks out. There's a negative response from his team. "Whoever it is, quit pissing around! If I find out who the asshole is, I'm going to wring your bloody neck!" The Leader warns. "Now get back to it!"

The team continues there task, treading cautiously through the debris field. Moments later, "It's a shame you're wasting all this effort for nothing." A ghostly sounding male voice now states. "Careful where you tread." It warns, followed by a reverberating laugh.

The team involuntarily stops in their tracks looking to the Team One Leader for direction, wondering if there is there something dangerous a foot. Speculating if this debris field is booby trapped…but how could that be possible after such an intense drone attack? Team OneLeader hand signals for all to hold their place and they cautiously scan for any hint of anything perilous as they wait for instruction.

"Team Three?" Team One Leader calls out to the larger force assigned to the bunker. "Are you picking up any strange transmissions?" He asks.

"Negative." Is the response. "What kind?"

"Weird voices." He replies.

"Negative."

"Team Two?" He calls to the ones searching what's left of the guest house. "Are you picking up any unusual chatter?"

"Negative." Is the answer.

"Command, are you picking up anything odd?" The Leader inquires.

"Negative," Is the reply. "What are you hearing?"

"Ah…not sure what to make of it, probably interference, we'll keep monitoring it and advise." Team One Leader says.

"Confirmed." Command answers.

"Okay, back at it." Team One Lead orders his group but fifteen minutes later, "Command, did we have confirmation the targets were on location at the time of the strike?" He asks.

"We had a verbal verification they were on site at zero five-fifteen, satellite corroborates no vehicles exited other than our agents inside. There was a visual of a target, probably female, leaving the main house for the bunker but it returned a few minutes later. There was no other activity or evidence of targets exiting the strike zone." Command replies.

"Affirmative." The Leader says.

"Better leave while you have a chance!" Unisons of soul-stirring male and female voices now loudly caution the team. Regardless of how experienced, tough and ruthless this mixed group of ex-military personnel are, these eerie happenings are having an effect. It's as if vengeful remnants of specters still remain among the wreckage.

"Alright…everybody…head sets off. Listen for my verbal commands and hand signals, enough of this bullshit." The Leader commands. It's obvious many of the team is getting unnerved.

"What the fuck is going on boss?" One of the team calls out.

Team One Lead gives him the middle finger so his message is obvious. "Shut the fuck up and keep looking!" He yells.

"This is strange shit." The member says quietly to the one near him.

"You got that." Is the hushed reply.

"We will never die!" The haunting voices suddenly scream out. "We will never die…never…never…ever die!! The voices shriek as they continue with their taunting, the volume increasing with every word, getting louder and louder with each repeated rendition. These eerie declarations become deafening and the increasing roaring, screeching sound of the voices immediately spreads from one Team One member to another like an air borne disease, and becomes so intense and high-pitched, it drops all of them to their knees. They press their hands hard against their ears to suppress the noise, to muffle the voices but to no avail. Some drop to fetal positions on the ground, bellowing and writhing in pain as blood seeps from their eardrums. Others have forced themselves to their feet, running blindly from the ruins, trying to distance themselves, hoping and praying for relief from the blaring heeds that are on the verge of driving them insane. The torture seems to go on for minutes but it has only been seconds and then…there's silence for them all.

Team Two, working the guest house site, witness the strange actions of Team One and rush to their aide as they're obviously experiencing some form of trauma. "Jesus Christ!" Team Two Leader shouts into his headset broadcasting to all the deployment teams including Command. "Command, Team One is down! I repeat Team One is down! We need choppers for immediate evac of casualties and possible transport out!" He motions to his team members. "Watch the perimeter!" And a select number of his team aims their weapons to the surrounding area as they advance, unsure if they're dealing with sniper fire or some other type of assault.

"Have they encountered hostiles?" Command asks.

"Negative!" Team Two Lead announces as he cautiously moves forward. "Negative! No visible hostiles identified!"

"What is the status of Team One?" Command requests.

"Unknown! Unknown!" Team Two Lead replies. "Will advice!"

"We are on our way for support!" Team Three Leader announces from the bunker.

"Negative." Orders Command. "Continue with your assigned mission."

"Repeat?" Team Three Lead requests.

"Negative on support for Team One and Two, hold your position and continue with your assigned mission." Command declares.

"Copy." Team Three Lead replies. He covers his mouthpiece. "Fucking assholes." As he turns to his subordinates in the vicinity, he releases his hold on the microphone, transmitting to all. "You heard Command, do what we're here to do!" He orders.

Half of Team One is wandering aimlessly, stumbling their way along, shouting for aide while the remaining members are still on the ground unable to recover from the ghostly audio assault. As Team Two approaches, those not assigned the task of guarding the perimeter, are shocked as they encounter their fellow comrades. There's visible bleeding from their ears and the blood vessels in their eyes have hemorrhaged transforming their orbs to a gory sight, their irises and pupils now surrounded by a dark red scarlet hue as a steady flow of drops of blood slowly escape and dribble down their cheeks. They soon realize their fellow compatriots are deaf and blind. Many look like zombies recently released from their graves as they wander, arms outstretched calling out for help as the scarlet red liquid escapes their orifices.

"Holy fuck!" A Team Two member shouts as he steps back from the path of one of the affected, not knowing if this a symptomatic condition of some disease, unsure if he should make any physical contact. "Boss!" He shouts. "What the fuck happened to them?! What do we do?"

Another Team Two member tries to grab hold of one of the female Team One group and she screams, flailing her arms in defense not knowing who or what she's encountered, having lost two of her critical senses. Team Two Lead rushes over and hugs her tight, holding her until she realizes she's in the arms of an ally, not someone she should fear. Other team members follow his lead, regardless of whether they are a man or a woman. Some of the comforting members weep quietly as they hold on tight, feeling helpless to further aid them.

"Command!" Team Two Lead spits out, taking a big breath to deflect the sob that is building in his throat, tears streaming down his face as he looks around at the others affected, each in the grasp of another. "Get those fucking choppers here now!" He sputters out. "They're all alive but down! I don't know what the fuck happened but it appears they've all lost their vision and hearing…fuck sakes." He sobs. He takes a few big breaths. "Command…what the hell do you have us chasing?!" But before a response can be made, two Chinook Helicopters come barreling into sight over the rise and seconds later land a hundred yards away. "Load em up!" Team Two Leader orders and as gently as they can, Team One is led to the waiting choppers. "Where are the medics?" Team Two Lead asks.

"Couldn't wait for them, they were fifteen minutes away and we didn't know the status of the casualties was so figured best to get them transported back ASAP." Is the crew member's reply. "What happened?" Team Two Leader shakes his head and waves him off, turning away, wiping away his tears without verbally responding and the helicopters lift off. Team Two gathers around their leader and they nervously scour the now barren area, there's not a sound not even a breath of wind. A feeling of isolation, of being defenseless begins to set in and they're unsure of what their next course of action should be.

"Team Two." Command calls out. The unexpected interruption of their paranoia startles most of them. "What is your status?"

Team Two Leader visually checks the faces of his team. "We're solid." He lies. "Team One was evacuated and away."

"Copy. Team Three, move out beyond the grounds to the woods west of the property and start a search. Our intelligence suggests that's the escape route our targets would have taken, to confirm, the woods west of the property. We'll dispatch a surveillance UAVs to assist. Team Two move into the bunker and keep it secured."

"Copy that." The Team Leaders confirm.

"Command is cold." A Team Two member mutters as they head to the bunker. "Ice cold."

Command switches to alternative channel used to communicate directly with the two dispatched Chinook rescue helicopters only. "Rescue one, come in?"

"Rescue One here, copy." The pilot replies.

"Orders from above; ascend to ten thousand feet, find an isolated location, strip your load and dump it." Command instructs.

"Repeat for verification." The pilot requests.

"Elevate to ten thousand feet, find a secure spot, strip and dump your cargo." Command orders.

"Affirmative." The pilot replies. "Bobby," The pilot transmits to the second helicopter's pilot. "You heard the man." The choppers reach the required altitude and hover over a dense peak of evergreens in the middle of nowhere. Team One has no idea what's coming as, one by one, the chopper crew stands them up and unceremoniously rips off their clothing, leaving them shivering in the frigid air, not caring if any scream or shout out as their comrades in the cabin with them, can't hear a word. They cower in the cold and can only feel the vibration of the chopper's rotors as they are led to the edge of the cabin, trusting that as they step out they'll be assisted and touching down on an asphalt pad…but there is no help, no solid footing, nothing but air. They do not see the trees as they pummel to the earth or hear the rush of the wind as they accelerate to a hundred and twenty miles per hour as they near the ground that will ultimately crush their bodies. For ten seconds they only feel the extreme cold with their descent, the feeling of utter helplessness and the wonder of what is actually happening to them before…they feel no more.

"Command," The helicopter pilots calls out. "The cargo has been delivered. To confirm, the cargo has been delivered."

"Copy." Replies Command.

The Male Voice Committee member has been monitoring all the communications of the operation and calls into Command directly via a landline. "Is it wise to send them Team Three into the woods?" It asks.

"We had confirmation the targets were on site and the search of the strike zones reveal no casualties and the bunker has been secured with none of the quarry being located. That's the only direction the targets could have gone undetected by the satellites. Do you want us to call off the pursuit, it's your operation?" Command answers.

The Male Voice ponders for a moment; it's getting nervous as there's now more at risk than it had initially bargained for or willing to sacrifice. "No, continue." It replies.

"No disrespect boss but what the fuck are we doing here, this was supposed to be a simple search and destroy?" A Team Two member asks as they make their way to the bunker. "Something is fucked up here…what exactly are we searching for?"

"Hey, what would you prefer? This or sitting on your ass at the base?" Team Two Leader asks.

"After seeing Team One, I'd rather be sitting on my fucking ass, safe and secure at base boss!"

"Too late." Team Two Leader answers. "Listen up and gather around!" He shouts as they approach the bunker stopping a hundred feet out giving space for Team Three, still exiting the bunker. "You!" He yells to a small grouping of his men. "Five of you guard the exterior entrances, another five take the garage and the rest move out to the bunker below! Our information shows that there are several wings in the bunker so as we enter the lower level, the first four in hold the rotunda, the rest of you to check each wing AGAIN and then maintain the corridors after the search is complete!"

"Didn't Team Three already do that?" A member calls out from the back.

"You're fucking lucky I can't see who said that!" Team Two Leader shouts back. "Otherwise I'd kick your ass down the entire four flights of stairs! Now move out!"

Team Three hurries to place charges on the twelve foot high, brick wall that surrounds the property to give them easy and direct access to the woods and seconds later, controlled blasts provides a massive opening for this force to move through but clearly displaying the towering and thick old-growth forest of pine, fir, cedar, spruce, oak and cottonwood with its multi-layered canopies they need to enter. The ground is layered with downed trees, logs and limbs and there's a heavy ground growth of fern, forbs, grasses and bushes.

"Listen Up!" Team Three Leader orders. "Same procedures and objective as before, we are looking for possibly eight targets…and they are badass…they have to be if they have this many sorry son of a bitches like us hunting for them. This is NOT a catch and detain mission! This IS a search and destroy! So be on guard. They've dispatched UAVs to assist but as you can see, they ain't gonna be much help. This is extremely difficult terrain with a lot of places to hide…keep your eyes sharp and up as well. Remember…we are also looking for a large globe shaped device about a foot in diameter which is a suspected nuclear device… DO NOT, I repeat, DO NOT attempt to handle it in any way, shape or form! Michaels, take the two flanked on either side of you and scout ahead of us, no further than one hundred yards! Everyone else spread out forming a line, keeping fifty feet between you! I want everyone to maintain a visual on the team member beside you at all times! Now move!" Its slow going and the deeper they penetrate, the more a closed in feeling becomes enhanced. There's a strong musky damp smell, the atmosphere is turning eerie and each obstacle becomes a potential ambush spot. Everyone's adrenalin is pumping, their senses are hyped.

The members of Team Two, with their interior search now complete, is anxiously waiting in the bunker monitoring the transmissions from Team Three who have the arduous task of maneuvering through the woods in their hunt and Team Two is not envious. The events of what just happened to Team One are still fresh in their mind and they're fearful about what Team Three may encounter out there.

"Michaels, report." Team Three Leader orders. There's no response from his scout team so he hand gestures for everyone to halt and the signal is passed down either side of the line. "Michaels, report." He repeats. Again, there's no reply. He hand signals for a cover position and follows this by signaling ten of the team to advance and recon.

"Team Three Leader, do you need back-up?" Team Two Leader transmits.

"Negative but we've lost contact with our scout team." Team Three Leader whispers into his headset. "I've sent a recon team."

"Copy." Team Two Leader says. "Command, did you receive the last transmission from Team Three?"

"Copy." Command answers.

The Male Voice is listening anxiously as the minutes go by. "Fuck." It whispers.

Ten minutes pass. "Recon team, report." Team Three Leader loudly whispers. There's no reply. "Shit." He mutters. His nearby team members indicate they want to advance but he shakes his head no and re-gestures for all to hold their positions. "Recon team, double-click if you can't verbally respond." Silence is the only answer. "Command, are the eyes in the sky picking up anything?"

"Negative." Command replies.

Team Three Leader bows his head in thought. Their targets might be playing them, purposely trying to draw them in a few at a time. Fourteen members may be down but if there's eight assailants and in this environment, than can easily be done. He may have been too cocky about sending out a scout team and then a recon, underestimating the capabilities of their targets but he was told they were civilians with no formal training…he's calling bullshit to that now. He still has close to a hundred and seventy-five strong, so he orders all to advance. "Command, we're moving in." He advises.

"Copy. Team Three Leader, be at the ready." Command orders.

Team Three Leader was right in his assumption, they're purposely being drawn in but it's not by their intended targets. The Tsiatko simultaneously emerge from the trees, from beneath large fallen logs, from the walls of the bunker, below ground and above…they are everywhere and everywhere at once. They outnumber the teams three to one. Those guarding the exterior of the bunker are dragged through the walls into the garage's interior as the other Tsiatko simultaneously seizes every one already in the bunker and in the dense forest…the teams have no opportunity to react, to call out or use their weapons. Brother has given his inhuman tribe permission to vent the thousands of years of pent up anger and revenge as they see fit and it's vicious; it's a slaughter. Some are wrapped up by the creatures' massive arms and squeezed until they burst like an inflatable figure. Others are seized by the throat, a fierce grip on their necks as the Tsiatko squeeze and release, threatening to crush it like it was a paper cup. The captive attempt to scream but it's to no avail because of the hold the creatures have. Those unfortunate to experience this, have no choice but to helplessly endure as the creatures bring their faces in close, their breath is rancid as they open their massive mouths, baring long menacing teeth and scream deafening, terrible howling snarls in their faces. Saliva spews out, covering the pinned members with thick dripping goo. After this brief taunting, the beasts squeeze tight and their victims' heads literally explodes off their bodies. Other team members are more fortunate and experience a swift end with Tsiatko simply stomping on their prey, swiftly converting them into pulpy masses while others are ripped apart or have their bodies repeatedly bashed against the trees, the bunker walls, the concrete floors. Regardless, they are all dying excruciating deaths. It's a bloody massacre that only lasts seconds. The creatures glare down at their enemies' carcasses, their chests heaving as they snarl and drool on the remains…the disdain and disgust they have for these pitiful excuses for flesh is indescribable.

Command can hear the vicious, animal like sounds. "Team Three, report." Command requests. "Team Three, report." There's no human reply, only the on-going echoing of savagery. "Team Two are you in contact with Team Three? All teams, report." No one answers, they can't. "Beale Base Command, are the UAVs picking up any kind of visual or sensor reading?"

"Negative." Beale Base replies.

"What the fuck was that?!" The Male Voice shouts.

"No idea and we've lost communication." Command answers.

"Yea, I get that! What the fuck now?!" The Male Voice demands.

"This is your operation. We can deploy more personnel but it'll have to be military. That's going to take time and people are going to ask why." Command answers.

"Shit!" The Male Voice answers.

"Heed us and bear witness!!" The creatures roar out in unison like a well rehearsed choir and the ear shattering announcement thunders through the trees and echoes into the nearby hills, reverberates through the few remaining operational headsets scattered about and is transmitted back to Command…to the Male Voice. The Tsiatko do not run away, they do not walk, they are strutting, moving with swagger and attitude as they depart because they've just declared that they are the superior race on this planet and this is their statement to all who dare to encroach or hunt them, that they are no longer taking the backseat to anyone or anything.

Somehow, Team Three Leader is alive, barely, his ribs are badly broken and have punctured a lung, his skull is fractured and one leg is shattered. He wipes away the blood from his eyes and painfully crawls to a headset that's still attached to a pulverized corpse. "Command?" He rasps out, coughing blood.

"Who is this?" Command asks.

"Team Three Leader." He replies wheezing.

"What's your status?" Command requests.

Team Three Leader sobs into the headset. "The Tsiatko…fuck man, you gotta get us out of here." He pleads not knowing he's the only survivor.

"Son of a bitch!" The Male Voice mutters.

The news of the failed mission spreads fast through the communication lines of the Committee and in a coordinated response; all the Committee members who voted for this operation, including the Male Voice are discreetly assassinated. Upon completion of this task, a secure landline rings at an unknown location in the U.S.

"Yes?" A woman answers.

"It's done." The caller confirms.

"Thank you." Ms. Olivia Rosalind Kinsey politely replies and hangs up. "Such incompetent fools." She adds, softly chuckling as she relaxes back in her Victorian fan chair and turns the TV volume back up.

CHAPTER FOURTENN

Its early morning, the sun has only been up for an hour or so, as Frank pulls into the parking lot of Mt. Rainier National Park. The place is already a hubbub of activity and he finds a corner spot that coincidentally faces the now sealed cavern opening, from where he and Zach made their escape, or in truth, the location they were permitted to breakout from. It's been three days since Frank left Lanesboro and his anger has been steadily increasing the more he has dwelt over the fact that he's being played…by everyone it seems. On his way here, he spent his nights in hotels so that he could take advantage of the guest computers to search for any information that would give him any hint of what may have happened, if anything, to the Handlers. The only thing he came across was a posting in the local Willow Creek news that mentioned the Humbug Creek Road, the very highway that led to the mansion grounds, was closed for construction and one other article discussing a military training exercise using a combination of air and ground personnel out of Beale Air Force Base in the Klamath National Forest west of Willow Creek at around the same…good old cover stories. He leaves the SUV idling, turns off the adult alternative radio station he's been listening to and crosses his arms on the steering wheel, so he can rest his chin in comfort as he stares away. Mt. Rainier's peak looks so peaceful but there's more than volcanic activity seething below its surface he suspects. He's back where all this crazy shit began. It's a place he once was in love with, now he's feeling slighted, like a spurned lover he's about to face once more even though Rainier itself had nothing to do with it. This place still reminds him of where he grew up, the wilderness side of it where he was free to do as he wished, back then and for awhile, here too…

oh, all the time he spent in these mountains, forests and valleys when he was a Deputy Sherriff.

It's the beginning of a great summer day, a cool one, perfect for the hike he's about to make but Frank's energy is waning, he's tired…maybe tired isn't the right description, it's his enthusiasm that's taking a hit. In the old days, what a fucking way to describe things…in the old days, Christ it's only been months but nothing is like it once was for him. He was retired, had a nice routine for himself, life was easy and now…fuck, he sees no light at the end of this tunnel. He sits back in his seat and shakes his head. He's been doing a lot of thinking the last few days as he was driving; the solitude of the road was good for him, always has been.

He exhales heavily. "Alright," He says out loud, "Get your ass in gear." He clambers out, swings open the rear driver's door, throws a cap on his now shaved bald head, zips up his jacket tight to his chin and flips up his collar. He dons a pair of round blue tinted hippy style sunglasses before examining his reflection in the window and smiles. Now that he's let his beard grow out again, he looks like he did in Belize and suddenly aches for the heat, sandy beaches and a warm ocean…he yearns for the taste of that salty sea water once again. Satisfied that he's unrecognizable as Deputy Frank Smirnov, he heads to the Ranger's Station to register his vehicle and notify them of his hike so as not to raise any red flags if he's late returning. The task done, he returns to his SUV, slips on a rucksack loaded with survival gear, a sleeping bag and a pup tent he picked up in Seattle enroute and heads out. Not that he intends to overnight but he knows he has to be prepared. He sets out at a jog; his destination is in a more remote area of the park, halfway to Gobbler's Knob where he first discovered Mr. H's cache with the aid of good old Stoner Oin and Silent Willow and shakes his head in amazement as to how easily he fell into the Handlers' ruse. He follows an old unused dirt and gravel road for four miles before he slows to a brisk walk, making his way to Lake George and its blue green waters. The views along the way are wondrous but he doesn't have the time to play tourist today…he's lying, he's ignoring the beauty as he doesn't want to be drawn back into it all, not here anyways. He has a task to complete…finish it and move on. He treks onward through open country and decides to take a break before beginning the steep climb through the old growth forest ahead of him. He finds a suitable boulder, has a drink and an instant breakfast meal. Out of habit, he checks the area below for any signs of movement although he's well aware he needn't bother checking his back trail as he knows other are probably doing that for him, he's sure his brethren are keeping a careful eye. He pulls a bag of weed and papers from his coat pocket, additional items he picked up during his pit stop in Seattle, and rolls a joint. He inhales deeply letting the weed do its thing, mellowing him, helping him clear his head and in no time, the cannabis is having the desired effect…maybe too much as he reluctantly rises. He moves on, through the dense woods of fir, cedar and hemlock that tower above him. He smells that familiar scent of dampness that envelopes the trees, feels the relaxing sounds of the wind humming through their branches and savors the sunlight gently filtering through from above, there is a sense of calm. He arrives at a large clearing in the thick of these woods, drops his knapsack to the ground and stretches before checking his watch, it's not even noon yet.

"My brother," Gaylord announces as he enters the clearing. "It is good to see you again." Gaylord's voice is deep but it doesn't have the same rumbling effect on him as Brother's. Brother's seems to penetrate through his body, engulfing him in sound and he wonders if it has something to do with his position as an Elder, something mystic that transformed it with that appointment.

"Gaylord, it's good to see you too. Is Brother nearby?" Frank asks.

"I am alone; we no longer occupy this mountain." Gaylord replies.

"But why?" Frank says.

"After the humans attacked and we took their spirits to defend ourselves, Brother believed it was no longer safe." Gaylord answers.

"I understand." Frank says. "Tell me, what's happened? Brother said the Orb was at risk. Are the Handlers okay?" Frank asks, unsure if he even really cares about their outcome, curiosity more than anything else.

"Here is the Orb." Gaylord replies, handing Frank a cloth wrapped bundle, its ends tied in a second knot to form a large handle so Gaylord could easily carry his precious cargo. "The Handlers are gone."

Frank sets the Orb down. "What do you mean gone?"

"Humans attacked the compound and destroyed the dwellings with," Gaylord hesitates. "I do not know the word…but they came in your flying machines, not planes, smaller…and helicopters and they fired powerful things that caused them to explode."

"Missiles, from drones?" Frank asks.

"Yes, that is what they were."

"Did the Handlers die?" Frank asks. "Willow?"

"No, I do not believe they perished but they are no more."

"What do you mean no more?" Frank says.

"Their bodies are no more, they are no longer here but their spirits remain."

"That makes no sense." Frank replies.

"That is all I know. That is all I saw." Gaylord replies.

"You saw?"

"Yes." Gaylord says.

"What did you see?"

"Willow came to me in the bunker where I was guarding the Orb as you had told me to. She came to warn me that an attack was coming very soon and that I must leave." Gaylord says as he looks down to the ground. "I told her that I already knew."

"What do you mean?"

Gaylord looks up. "I told her I knew the attack was coming and that I had already moved the Orb to safety. I could see by the way she looked at me, she knew she had been betrayed. She gave me this," And Gaylord opens the palm of his immense hand and reveals a flash drive to Frank. "To give to you and to tell you she is not sure if she will ever see you again and everything you would need to know is in this."

Frank picks up the flash drive. "Betrayed by who and what became of her?" He demands.

"She went back to the dwelling and then they came…and after, the Handlers were no longer there." He does not reveal what happened to the teams that were on the ground following the attack on the Handlers, what their fate was at the hands of the Tsiatko.

Frank stares at the memory stick. "Who betrayed her?"

Gaylord gazes around before answering. "It is not for me to say." He states.

Frank shoves Gaylord, it's like pushing against a brick wall and he doesn't budge. "Goddamn it! Tell me what you know!"

Gaylord scans the area once more. "It is not my place." He whispers loudly.

Frank understands now, Gaylord must fear confessing what he knows, afraid of being overheard even though there should be no other Tsiatko here so Frank comes in close. "I am your brethren and you are mine." Frank whispers. "We have shared the battlefield and we fight a common enemy…I must know, you have to tell me." Frank sees that Gaylord is still struggling; he's torn as to where his allegiances should be.

"If I tell you…" Gaylord mutters.

"I have learned much from the Orb." Franks says. "If this path continues, no one will win and the Tsiatko may suffer the most. This I can tell you with a true heart. I am not asking you to betray him; I'm begging you to trust me." He pleads.

Gaylord's eyes shift from the ground and back to Frank several times. Frank doesn't want to push him and lets him mull it over. Frank grabs Gaylord's arm. "Trust me, my brother because… I will never betray you."

"It was…Brother who betrayed the Handlers." Gaylord confesses.

Frank is dumbfounded and steps back. "What?!" He says.

Gaylord moves forward. "Do not fail me, you promised." Gaylord whispers. "It was with a human woman…one he has known and met for many, many years."

Frank leads Gaylord to the center of the clearing, distancing themselves from the trees. "A Handler?" Frank asks.

"I do not believe so. She is very old now, for a human."

"You have seen her, seen them meet?" Frank says.

"Yes. I have escorted Brother whenever they have met. They have planned together before. I do not know all they have done; Brother always said it was what was best for the Tsiatko."

"What have they done before?" Frank asks.

"I do not know." Gaylord lies.

"Do you know her name?"

Gaylord is still for a moment. "Brother calls her Olivia." He finally reveals.

"Olivia, Olivia what?" Frank asks, still whispering.

"I do not understand." Gaylord asks.

Frank is a bit exasperated. "Humans usually have two names, a first and a last. My human last name is Smirnov."

"Frank…Smirnov." Gaylord repeats.

"Yes. Did this human woman have another name besides Olivia?"

"I do not know. I only know Olivia." Gaylord answers.

"Shit." Frank replies. He shoves the USB that he unknowingly has a death grip on, in his pant pocket and begins to pace. "Can't fucking trust anyone." He mumbles. He eventually stops and extracts the memory stick as Willow's message repeats in his head. "Everything you need to know is in this." Is the USB a lead to Olivia or is he being played some more? Either way, he'll need a computer. "Gaylord, I must go. Thank you, my brother." Frank says and leaves Gaylord where he stands. Frank cautiously hurries his descent, hoping to get down before dark to avoid any missteps and possible injury which is the last thing he needs. The sun is just going down as he arrives at the road he first took on the way up so he slows to a walk, just four miles to go. As he nears the parking lot, he stops… something isn't right. As he peers through the line of trees, separating him from his destination a hundred yards away, he removes his silencer equipped Glock from his shoulder holster. The moon is in a waxing crescent phase, not enough to illuminate the night and give him a clear view of everything but at the same time, sufficient enough to keep him concealed in the dark. He crouches down and listens. The cool air carries sound well…and that's what caught his attention, the quiet. The park, officially, should still be open but there are no voices, no sound of vehicles, nothing. He's wishing he hadn't abandoned Gaylord so quickly. He creeps closer, moving fifty feet at a time before pausing to check for unseen assailants until he reaches the lot's perimeter. His SUV is where he left it and appears unscathed. There is one other vehicle, a white Bronco, parked near the Ranger's Station and a light is on inside the building. The highway entry lights are lit up and he can see that the chain is across the entrance which usually means there's a locked padlock securing it in place. "Shit." He mutters as he moves to his SUV… maybe he fucked up on the hours. He's not sure how to proceed, bust through the chain knowing the Ranger's have his plate number or see who's in the office to let him out? He's quietly climbs in his vehicle, not worried about being illuminated as he always shuts off the interior cabin light control and tosses the knapsack on the passenger seat before placing the automatic on his lap. As he looks up, he finds the answer to his dilemma staring back at him. There's a note tucked under the wiper with the writing facing him — Frank we need to talk Ranger's Office — He quickly exits, ducking down leaving the rucksack where it lay and gently closes the door. He locks it with the fob as he moves to the rear of the SUV, letting it give him as much cover as possible and pats his jacket to verify his spare loaded clips are still where they should be. He surveys the lot before sprinting to the Bronco. He feels his adrenalin pumping, his senses are heightening, his eyes are turning enhancing his natural night vision…he's in battle mode. He approaches a window in the station and quickly peeps in, there's a sole figure obviously a man, facing away from him seated at a desk behind the counter wearing a wide brimmed hat with his jacket hanging off the back of the chair. He checks the interior once more, there's no one else. He scouts the entire exterior of the building, listening, looking outward for any signs of an ambush and can find none. He moves near the front entrance before resting back against the wall, he relaxes, not having discovered any imminent danger and he feels his eyes returning to normal. "What the fuck is going on?" He mutters. He tests the lock…its open and so he enters.

"Hey Frank." His old boss, Sherriff Barton says. He's leaning back in the chair, arms crossed on his chest, his cowboy boot covered feet propped up on the desk with his issued felt campaign hat tipped back on his head.

Frank remains by the door, his weapon hanging by his side as he looks around.

"Ain't nobody else here but us chickens." The Sherriff laughs. He has a smug look on his face.

His words make Frank think of Zach, with his fox in the henhouse look that Frank experienced the first time they met…well, when he first met him as Agent Zachariah Allmass not as his old boyhood schoolmate, Adam Pope. "How'd you know I was here…and you don't seem too surprised that I am here and alive?" Frank says.

"Nope." The Sherriff replies, offering no other information. He suddenly swings his feet down, sliding in close to the desk on the casters of the chair.

Frank aims his Glock at the Sherriff.

"No need for that son." The Sherriff says, slowing raising his hands, his face turning pale.

"Keep your hands up and roll off to the side, away from the desk." Frank orders. The Sherriff does as he's told. "Now slowly stand and turn in a circle."

Barton complies, knowing Frank wants to verify he's unarmed. With the aid of his slender arms, the seventy-five year old Sherriff pushes his skinny, pot bellied six foot frame out of the chair and stands on stick-like legs. He would not be considered a physically fit or menacing individual.

Frank walks over to check under the desk for any concealed weapons. "Alright," Frank says. "Sit back down, stay where you are and keep your hands on the arm rests."

"You got it son."

Frank lowers the Glock; he worked with the Sherriff for two years in Ashford before Fate came a calling to whisk him away on his crazy adventure leaving around here thinking he's dead. The Sherriff's sitting here like nothing happened. "What the fuck is this?" Frank asks.

"Well, there's a pretty important individual who carries a lot of clout and influence who wants to talk to you and she asked me to set it up." Barton says.

"She?"

"Yes. Ms. Olivia Rosalind Kinsey." Barton announces like the name is supposed to mean something to Frank. It does, only because that's the same first name of the woman Gaylord just told him about. Son of a bitch, he's being played again…fucking Gaylord too? Frank approaches Barton letting his eyes go dark. "This is bullshit. Fuck you and fuck your Ms. Kinsey!"

"Jesus Christ!" Barton says, pushing himself away in the chair. "What the hell are you?"

Frank marches in closer, clamping down on Barton's hands that seem glued to the arm rests, pressing his entire weight down on them and brings his face in close so they are eye to eye, letting Barton clearly experience the frightful looking dark orbs that were once his grey eyes. "I'm a guy who hates games." He states pushing away hard sending Barton slamming into the wall.

Barton's his hat tumbles off his head falling behind the chair exposing his comb-over, the long thin hairs now falling forward over his face and he leaves them where they lay, he's in pain but doesn't dare move. "This…this ain't no game son!"

Frank aims his weapon at Barton. "This whole fucking thing is one big game and I'm not playing anymore."

Barton is scared, it's plain to see. "Look Frank, I have no idea what you're talking about. I'm just doing as I'm told."

"By this Ms. Kinsey." Frank says sarcastically.

"Yea, I mean…you must know her? Goddamn it, she's the one who recommended I hire you in the first place. Said she knew you quite well, would be a definite asset to the team and you were!" Barton says. "I swear!"

Frank lowers his gun, he believes him but who the hell is this woman? "And how do you know her?" He asks.

"Well…you could say we have some history. I've been doing her favors every now and then ever since I began in law enforcement. The pay she was offering back then definitely helped my retirement fund." He confesses. "Now, she still pays well but I do it more because I want to."

"Oh, you're a bit sweet on her are you?"

"Sure I have feelings for her, she's a good woman." Barton admits, blushing slightly. "But I know she's outta my league so I just do what I do for her."

"Well, if she's so influential and you have done so much for her, why are you still just a Sherriff?" Frank asks, challenging him.

Barton is leaving his hands in place but opening and closing them trying to reduce the throbbing pain he's still experiencing. "You know, most people don't know their limitations, me, I do. I'm not cut out to be a big dog son, I'm quite happy being a little old Sherriff here in Ashford."

"So where and when am I to meet your Ms. Kinsey?" Frank asks.

Barton shakes his head. "I can't tell you that Frank. I'm supposed to take you there." He replies boldly.

"Is that what she told you to tell me if I asked?"

Barton looks surprised. "How'd you know that?" He asks warily.

Frank laughs. "Does Ms. Kinsey share your feelings; think you two are pretty tight?"

"What's so funny? I think she may." Barton says, sounding offended.

Frank shakes his head and smiles. "Well, hate to break it to you; you're going to be disappointed about how she truly feels about you, not that she's going to tell you herself. I would say Ms. Kinsey may know me after all, better than you at least, because the Frank standing before you is not the Frank that worked for you. If you actually knew the real me, you wouldn't be sitting here all alone, unarmed and give me that kind of an answer." He says. "What I don't understand is why people feel they have to go through all this drama just to talk to me, first Allmass and his Belize fiasco and now Kinsey with you." He adds muttering.

"What's Agent Allmass got to do with this?"

"Huh, oh, just talking out loud." Frank says approaching Barton, clamping down on his shoulder as he presses the end of the silencer tight against one of the Barton's hand and fires a round. The shell penetrates his hand, the arm rest and splinters the wooden floor followed by a cascade of blood from the wound.

Barton screams as he tries to get up but Frank holds him in place and shoves the weapon in his open mouth, breaking a tooth and stifling his wailing. Barton presses his wounded hand hard against his chest trying to stop the flow of blood and a crimson stain slowly engulfs the front of his shirt as scarlet dribble flows over his lips and down his chin.

"Don't utter another sound Sherriff." Frank whispers in his ear. "The pain you're feeling is only the beginning if you don't answer my questions, I can do this all night long. Understand?"

Barton, his pupils enlarged, tears streaming down his face, nods in agreement.

Frank removes the Glock from his mouth, wiping off the barrel on Barton's pant leg.

"Where and when are we supposed to meet?" Frank asks.

Barton coughs and spits blood on the floor. "She has a penthouse in Seattle. She didn't give a day or time because she wasn't sure how cooperative you'd be." Barton sobs, rocking back and forth in the chair, his wounded hand still pressed tight against his chest. "I told her I could convince you to come. I was supposed to call to let her know when we were on the way."

"Look at that, you've convinced me. What's her number and the address?"

"It's in my phone, sitting on the desk there." Barton answers.

"Don't move Sherriff." Frank warns as he walks to the desk, his weapon still trained on him. Frank picks it up. "Is there a password?"

Barton shakes his head no.

What's she under?"

"Olivia." Barton spits out.

Frank opens the contact list and confirms the information before powering it off. Without any adieu, he shoots Barton in the head followed by two in the chest. He walks over, checks for a pulse and picks up his brass before heading for the door. He doesn't bother wiping anything down as there's probably hundreds of prints scattered inside here, good luck sorting them out. His rental vehicle...he's got time, he'll dump it in the morning along with the gun as neither can be traced back to him. He stops mid-step and turns back to search the pockets of Barton's jacket, firmly held in place on the chair by the lifeless body slumped in it. He finds what he's looking for, keys, one of which should be for the chained entry gate and leaves, shutting off the light and locking the door behind him. He pauses outside the door, checking the area once more and suddenly Gaylord emerges from the night. "What are you doing here?" Frank demands.

"I followed you, and when I saw you come to this dwelling, I watched and listened through the window." Gaylord replies. "…and I saw you take that human's spirit."

"Why did you tell me about Olivia?" Frank asks. "Did Brother instruct you too?"

"No." Gaylord says.

"Then why?" Frank asks again.

There is little light but enough for Frank to see Gaylord's face has a puzzled expression. "I did because you asked me to, do you not remember, Frank Smirnov?"

"Why are you calling me that?"

"Because that is your name." Gaylord says in a matter of fact tone.

"Why not before?" Frank replies.

"I did not because you never told me your name; I only heard it through others, so I believed it would be offensive for me to do so." Gaylord says.

Frank can't argue with that even though at times he feels he's having a discussion with a child but he knows Gaylord, like all the Tsiatko, are highly intellectual Beings and their logic and rational is beyond most people's comprehension and, he even though he no longer trusts Brother, his gut says trust Gaylord. Trust no one, Mr. H's suddenly warning rings out again, haunting him. How true that has become and he wonders if the warning should include Mr. H himself. Was he part of the conspiracy to control Frank or did things change from an original plan he may have had when he disappeared from Roswell with the Orb. Maybe it all took a turn when he handed the Orb over to the Tsiatko, Frank probably will never know. Right now he wishes he knew why Olivia Kinsey was reaching out to him. "You remember the city where you, Oin, Zach and I traveled to in the van; can you go there on your own?" Frank asks hesitantly.

"I have been there before." Gaylord states.

"You have?" Frank answers surprised.

Gaylord laughs. "We are not animals that fear humans, we only fear your technology and dread discovery; we have visited your towns and cities over the ages, out of curiosity and necessity. I have been to your Seattle many times." He says.

"Oh," Frank says. "Do you understand a map?"

"Yes, Frank Smirnov, I understand what a map is and yes, I can follow one too." Gaylord replies smiling.

"Hey, sorry, just when I think of you living your life out here, I don't expect you to know much of our, I mean, the human world." Frank turns and kicks in the door of the Ranger's office before remembering he has Barton's keys. "Hang on." Frank says as he turns on a light.

"To what?" Gaylord asks.

Frank shakes his head. "Never mind, just wait here a moment." And he heads to the counter to see if there's a map of Seattle, his hunt is unsuccessful and so he exits. "I'll be right back." He says and sprints to his SUV, avoiding the parking lot lights and retrieves a map of Seattle from the glove box. He had picked up as he's still paranoid about being tracked electronically by phone or even vehicle and had disconnected the GPS system on the SUV shortly after he pulled out of the rental lot. He runs back to the office, moves past Gaylord and grabs a few thumbtacks off a notice board inside before switching on the exterior light and heading out. He opens the map, pins it to the wood exterior wall so Gaylord can clearly view it and powers up Barton's phone…Olivia is downtown at the Kompton Milan Hotel, as all the high-end hotels seem to be. Its listed and numbered on the map and it only takes him a few moments to locate it. "Man, I wish you could tell time." Franks says.

Gaylord places his hand on Frank's shoulder. "We can tell time, my brethren. Do you remember that day Brother gave us his words of wisdom in the cavern, it was when you discovered through the Orb what the Handlers had done to ensure the humans' survival on this world?" Gaylord doesn't wait for a response. "As Brother had said, the Tsiatko have been on this world since the beginning, the beginning plus a day and we speak all your languages even those that have been lost to time. We can do that because Brother taught us to know our enemies in order to defeat them and the Tsiako do consider humans to be our adversaries." He says.

Frank has to remind himself that the Tsiatko do not think of him as human but one of them and so Gaylord's words are not meant to offend or threaten him.

"And so we have studied the humans, we know all there is to their ways. The Tsiatko have witnessed that humans cannot live in harmony with anything, even themselves and will ultimately cause the destruction of this world, the very place we hold so sacred, our home; we will no longer permit this. And when they are gone, we will not be living in their modern dwellings or driving their automobiles, we have no desire to soar in the sky in their flying machines, we will live and exist as we have for thousands of years, out here with Mother Earth because we choose to do so, not that we have to. I tell you all this Frank Smirnov to help you understand that a new age is coming, the age of the Tsiatko and this transition has already begun. I tell you this so you will not fear what is about to come as you are one of us, you are Tsiatko. I am assisting you because you are my brethren and you are battling these humans. It does not matter if this human Olivia must one day fall at your hands or the Tsiatko as it is all the same hand, she has used the Tsiatko's to her advantage the same as we have used her, as we have done with the Handlers." Gaylord confesses.

Frank is dumbfounded, never has Gaylord spoke with such openness and insight. Frank feels foolish thinking of him as nothing more than a primitive soldier in the Tsiatko's battle. It's clear he's much more and probably all the Tsiatko fit this profile. "What did you mean by, it has begun?" He asks.

Gaylord softly pats Frank's shoulder and smiles. "Show me Frank Smirnov, where and when you need me to be." He says.

After Frank coordinates things with Gaylord, he strolls to his SUV, ignores the parking lights and doesn't bother checking his back as he goes. Once in, he powers up Barton's cell, jots down Ms. Kinsey's information then removes the SIM card, breaks it in two and removes the cell's battery. He drives to the gate, headlights off and checks the highway before removing the chain. He tosses Barton's keys, the cell, its battery and SIM card halves into the marshy, water laden ditch and clambers back in his vehicle. It's only seventy miles to Seattle so plenty of time to find an Internet café to check Willow's flash drive, from there, who knows.

He locates one on Northgate Way that's open twenty-four seven and two hours later, Frank rubs his eyes before leaning back in his chair, a café latte in his hand. The computer screen is getting to him and he takes a sip of the espresso that he considers a treat. He's been pouring through all the information on Willow's USB, the data is pretty comprehensive on the Committee with most of the intelligence related to their current operations. He doesn't give a fuck about them right now; he just wanted to find something on this Olivia Rosalind Kinsey. He did come across a brief reference to her, that she once was the matriarch, the powerful head of the Committee but she stepped down from that position quite some time ago. Frank believes otherwise…she's still pulling the strings, his included somehow. Frank does think he has an edge though, one that none should be aware of; ever since he started syncing with the Orb, his perspective has changed. For him it's not about the Committee, the Handlers, the Tsiatko…he's not even sure it's about every human being on this planet anymore because he's looking at things on a grander scale now. Now it's about finishing the job Mr. H gave him, he's undertaken the responsibility of the Orb and all that goes with it same as when he accepts a hit; he sees it through to the end and his version of how things should now conclude will not be welcomed by any. This Kinsey woman appears to be someone who may be standing in his way. If not, she's definitely an obstacle. He sets down his drink and pulls out the note tucked away in his shirt pocket — The Kompton Milan Hotel on 4th Avenue — where Kinsey is supposed to waiting for him…well, if she is, she's going to be waiting a bit longer.

CHAPTER FIFTEEN

Frank groans as he turns on his side, reluctantly opening his eyes and it takes him a moment to remember where he is…the Comfort Inn near the Seattle airport. He died last night but a big part of that had to do with the hefty joint he smoked before bed, without it, his mind would have been racing, planning things over and over again in his head…working out every scenario and he wouldn't have slept a wink. The weed is the only thing that helps him shut everything out without any dire consequences the next day. He lies on to his back and stares up at the stippled white ceiling, contemplating the busy day he has ahead. He had dumped the Glock he used on Sherriff Barton along with the expended brass in Lake Union last night and this morning, the SUV needs to disappear. He sits up, swinging his feet to the floor and checks that his sports bag, duffle bag, knapsack and banker box are where he left them by the door…involuntary paranoia. He should burn the box of documents Zach had stashed away in Glenford but he can't, not yet anyways. He walks to it, crouches down and flips off its lid. He extracts the photograph he tucked away in it, staring at the image, still lost as to what their endgame was…is. He tosses the picture back in, grabs Willow's flash drive off the table, where he placed it after he emptied his pockets last night, throws it in as well and presses the cover back on tight, out of sight, out of mind. He quickly showers and puts on the only clean thing he has, black cargo pants, red t-shirt and a black flight jacket. Not exactly the look he wants but it'll have to do. He exits the room, re-checking the lock and heads downstairs, as he nears the main level he throws on a black baseball cap and shades and makes his way for the complimentary continental breakfast. He knows he has to eat and a couple cups of coffee to get him kick started, caffeine actually, his morning mainstay.

That done, he drives to a Sud's full service carwash and selects the "Total Car Care Package". Two hours and three hundred dollars later the SUV is spotless, inside and out, scrubbed clean as he waited in their lounge and indulged in more of the hearty brew that awakens him each and every morning. Now, he's on his way to the airport where he enters the Park N Jet; pays for a month of parking and stows the SUV deep among a slew of other vehicles. After wiping down the door and steering wheel, he takes the six minute shuttle ride to the terminal and locates the terminal map, searching for car rental agency locations, a very specific one. He moves on through the terminal and turns off the main corridor, across polished brown slate tiles, through a line of display luxury vehicles including Porsche, Bentley, Land Rover, Audi and Ferrari and pushes through frosted glass doors into a large kiosk, home to the Enterprise Air Port Exotic Car Rental office, removing his sunglasses as he enters. The male attendant behind the counter has slicked back blonde hair, too dark a tan, teeth that are way too white, dressed in a navy blue tailored suit, an open collar baby blue dress shirt, with gold chains hanging off his neck and a heavy gold bracelet drooping off his wrist…the guy looks like a sleazy salesman.

"Can I help you sir?" He asks snidely as Frank approaches.

"What do you have in the way of Mercedes?" Frank asks.

"Um," The attendant is hesitant to answer, probably based on Frank's appearance. "Are you sure this is where you want to be?" He asks.

Frank stares at him with cold grey eyes as he reaches into his inside jacket pocket and removes a brown Louis Vuitton card holder, exhibiting an array of platinum credit cards. He removes a U.S. Bank Visa and slides it across the counter to the agent. The display achieves the desired effect.

"Of course," The agent replies all smiles as he picks up the card. "…Mr. Elliot. Let me check our inventory. One moment please." As he keys information into the desktop. "Uh, we have a black AMG GT Roadster? Will that work?"

"Perfect." Frank replies. "I'll need it for a couple weeks."

The attendant is beaming now. "You have great taste Mr. Elliot, excellent choice." He replies.

Thirty minutes later, Frank floors the two door convertible coupe with its handcrafted V8 turbo, five hundred and fifty horsepower engine and in three point seven seconds; he's doing sixty miles per hour. He laughs, enjoying the thrill of the ride, it's not his cherished 300SE he had to abandon in Ashford but it'll do. Forty-five minutes later, he screeches to a halt in front of Bottler & Renwick's Men's Shoppe on Union Street and struts in through the clear glass double entrance door. He holds his hand up, hushing the impeccably dressed sales person who's about to speak as he enters and makes his way to the suit section of the retailer. He browses through the rack as the sales clerk quietly follows him unsure how to react and waves over, what must be a manager, also well clothed. Frank selects a Italian made navy linen two piece suit and lays it out on a table followed by a English made black fresco suit, a black Louis Vuitton western cut suit and a half dozen white Canclini cloth French cuff dress shirts. He explores the store further and picks a pair of tiger black toe cap oxford dress shoes, black Firenze half brogue oxfords and black Bergamo monk strand shoes, which he adds to the pile. He wraps things up by choosing a dozen pair of colorful dress socks, six paisley pocket squares and three sets of cufflinks in rectangle, crown and stepped designs plus twelve pairs of boxer style briefs. He reviews his collection before selecting a couple black belts and two pairs of suspenders. "That should be it." He announces.

The clerk and manager are a bit dumbfounded. "I'm impressed sir. When would you like these for?" The manager asks.

"End of the day." Frank replies.

The clerk interrupts, chuckling. "Impossible sir…the typical time to have these suits and shirts tailored for you is two to three weeks."

Frank extracts a wad of C-notes and quietly counts out five thousand dollars and throws it on top of the pile. "Will that cover expediting this?" Frank asks.

The manager checks around before picking up the bills to count them, looking at Frank once he's confirmed the amount. "Yes sir, it will." He says smiling, tucking the cash away inside his sports coat.

"I had hoped so." Frank says. "I need these delivered by the end of the day to the Kompton Milan downtown where I'll be staying. Are you familiar with it?"

"Of course, Mr.?" The manager replies.

"Elliot, Richard Elliot." Frank answers.

"And how will you be paying?" The manager asks.

"Credit card." Frank states as he selects another platinum one from his assortment.

The manager passes the card to the clerk. "Process Mr. Elliot's transactions while I personally measure him up." He orders. "Please, follow me Mr. Elliot." He adds.

That task completed, Frank walks one block over to a well-rated barber shop for a hot towel, straight razor shave for his bald head and a square cut trim for his ever graying beard, keeping as much of the length as possible. An hour later, Frank is back in the Roadster, heading downtown to the Kompton…he needs to surveil this Olivia Kinsey and he'd decided he's going to do it in plain sight so he needs to look the part, clothes and ride. The Kompton Milan is tucked right in the thick of things amongst the Pike Place Market, Pioneer Square, the 5th Avenue Theatre, the Sports Stadium and a short walk away from the water front. He turns down 4th Avenue and a block later he pulls up to a grand looking ten-story and stops at its groovy looking, red and yellow striped awning. A twenty-something valet along with a even younger looking porter, immediately come rushing out to greet him. Frank pops the remote trunk before getting out and tossing the valet the keys. "I'll take the sports bag; the rest can go on a luggage cart." He says.

"Yes sir, sweet ride." The valet exclaims smiling.

Frank grabs the sport bag which contains the Orb. "It's a rental, so have some fun if you want." He announces handing the valet a fifty, who provides him with a parking stub. The valet grins; he can't help but show his excitement at the prospect.

"Do you have a reservation sir?" The porter inquires visibly displaying his jealousy of the porter's pending joy ride.

"No." Frank replies.

"Follow me please." The porter says and leads the way to the front desk.

Frank pauses as he enters, struck by the eye catching and funky art deco style. He's gazes at the immense art filled lobby with its twenty-two foot ceilings and elaborate crystal laden chandeliers hanging down among tall, square stately pillars like clusters of clear grapes. Homey lounging areas, each with its own wood burning marble mantled fireplace, are strategically placed decorated in palettes of grey, light blues, reds and creams. He moves inward and is amazed by the over-all vibe, more so as he passes an unconventional dolphin mural encompassing an entire wall which reminds of the Mediterranean. He's impressed.

"Good day sir, welcome to the Kompton Milan." The female front desk clerk says. "Do you have a reservation?"

"No." Frank says.

"How long will you be staying with us?" The desk clerk asks.

"Not sure, a week, possibly longer." Frank states.

"Have you stayed at any of our Kompton properties before?"

"No." Frank says.

"Very good sir, do you have a preference for a room?" She inquires.

"Something roomy, king size bed and with a view."

Of course sir, one moment, let me check what I have available." The clerk replies as she checks the availability of the various rooms. "Okay…I have a corner suite with a view of the bay for four hundred and eighty a night?"

"That will be just fine." Frank replies handing over a credit card.

She scans his card and momentarily passes him two magnetic keys. "Is there anything else we can do for you at this time Mr. Elliot?" She asks.

"Yes, there is. I'm expecting a wardrobe delivery from Bottler & Renwick's later in the day, can it be brought up?"

"Of course Mr. Elliot, consider it done and enjoy your stay. If there's anything you need, please don't hesitate to call the front desk or our concierge service." She replies. "The contact information for those and any of our other services and amenities, you'll find in the information brochure in your room."

"Thank you." Frank says. "Oh…I should have asked, do you have penthouse suites?"

"We do Mr. Elliot, four of them. Unfortunately two are permanently rented to private parties and the other two are currently taken." She replies.

"Is there any possibility of viewing the permanently rented ones, if there empty, so I have an idea for next time?" Frank asks.

"I'm sorry but those parties are currently occupying those units and I wouldn't be able to ever show those particular suites regardless." She replies.

"I understand, maybe on my return trip." Frank answers.

"We would be more than happy to have you view the other ones if their open." She replies smiling.

"This way please, Mr. Elliot." The porter instructs and leads Frank to the guest elevator as he pushes the luggage cart. As they elevator goes up, Frank tries to assess this uniformed kid riding up with him who's staring straight ahead. He's young, clean cut, slim, of average height with dark hair but his assessment must have been too obvious or interpreted as something else. The porter turns to him. "Is something wrong Mr. Elliot?" He asks.

"Pardon?" Frank asks.

"Um, not to offend you…you've been staring at me; I can see that in the door's reflection." He says and with that, the elevator opens on his floor. The kid exits and makes his way to Frank's room, the first one on the right and swipes the magnetic pad with his master pass card, holding it open for the approaching Frank. Frank takes notice that the hallways are monitored by ceiling mounted cameras as he makes his way to his room and enters. Frank holds the door open as the kid pushes in the cart, closes it and appears to stand guard. The kid glances back and turns to face Frank as he nervously looks around, he's visibly troubled by Frank's actions.

'Take it easy." Frank says. "I'm not gonna hurt you or anything, just need some information."

"….Sure." The kid replies. "I'm new here, only three months but I'll tell you what I can."

"What's your name?" Frank asks.

The kid points to the name tag pinned on his chest. "Samuel." He says. "Sam for short."

Frank laughs at his own oversight and Samuel appears to relax a bit. Frank strips off a C-note and hands it to him. "How old are you?" He says.

"Twenty-one Mr. Elliot." Samuel answers as he reluctantly takes the money. I'm mean, the cash is appreciated but I really don't know much, not that I have any idea what you want."

"It's simple kid. I have a tentative business meeting with Ms. Olivia Kinsey in a week and I know she has a penthouse suite here. That's why I was asking about them at the front desk, to confirm she's around but I have no idea what she looks like as we've never met before. I don't want to look like a fool if I accidently bump into her before the meeting so I'm hoping you can help me out." Frank says.

"What, like point her out?" Samuel asks.

"No, better, I want you to discreetly take a picture of her." Frank answers.

Samuel smiles. "Hey man; that I can do. I'll probably see her later today, I'm on shift; will that work?"

"That'd be great." Frank says as he props open the door. "Just put my stuff on the floor and get out of here. I don't want to be wasting anymore of your time."

Samuel tucks the hundred dollar bill in his pants pocket. "Mr. Elliot, with what you're paying me, you're not wasting my time; consider it done and if you need anything else, just let me know." He answers grinning as he pushes the cart out the door and it automatically closes behind him with Frank's release.

Frank quickly re-opens it. "Hey Sam," He calls out; he checks that the hallway is empty. "Just between us, okay?"

Sam gives a thumb up sign and keeps moving.

Frank turns back into the room and it's his first chance to actually view his accommodations as he was distracted by the task of recruiting Sam and he's as pleasantly surprised as when he entered the lobby. The first thing that strikes him is the calming colors of brown, creams and light blues throughout that are accented by splashes of red and royal blue using carefully thought out trappings. He walks through the main space which features a living area with a full couch and two armchairs, a large wall mounted TV, a wood burning fireplace, dining area, a collection of art and books and makes his way to one of the corner floor to ceiling windows which provides a full view of the bay. The sight reminds him of the Golden Gate Bridge that he could see from the three-level home he had in San Francisco up on Russian Hill and with those memories; it stirs up the pangs of loss for only love, violently taken from him. Fucking emotions…and he shrugs it off. He walks past the centered patio doors leading to a balcony and finds, hidden behind frosted etched glass French doors, a huge bedroom with more wall to ceiling views, another fireplace, a king size bed holding a multitude of plush pillows tucked away in an array of decorative accent covers and a matching goose down comforter. Belgium chocolates fill a tray on the night stand and he grabs one as he heads to the adjoining washroom to discover a deep jetted tub, a walk-in glass shower, Italian Frette linens and luxury Atelier Bloem bath amenities. He savors the creamy rich edible as it melts in his mouth; he thinks he's going to enjoy it here.

Later that evening, Frank is on the couch, his bare feet propped up on the coffee table near an open bottle of Pellegrino as he reads a complimentary copy of The Seattle Times. He misses reading, he use to do so much; especially something he can lay his hands on, even a newspaper. There's something enjoyable about the feel of paper, the scent of the ink and the sensation of turning a page. He looks over at the dining room table where the his recently finished room service meal is scattered and its aroma still fills the air; clam escabeche for an appetizer, followed by a field green salad, black Chile roasted duck and a rich vanilla cheesecake for dessert. He has the TV on a music video channel and he's savoring it all, the touch, the sounds, the visual sensations, he's in his zone…it's been too long. The door bell rings, interrupting his bliss and he chuckles, a fucking door bell. He gets up to check the door and since he's not one to check the peep hole since he's put too many of his prey down that way, he stands to the side of the door and cracks it slightly to see who's there, it's Samuel.

"I have your delivery Mr. Elliot." Sam announces.

Frank swings the door open and Sam pushes in a birdcage luggage cart loaded with Frank's purchase from Bottler & Renwick. "Just park that to the side and I'll empty it later." Frank says.

"You got it boss." Sam replies and does as he's instructed. "Hey," As he reaches into his pocket and takes out his cell phone. "I got what you asked for."

"You got the pictures already?" Frank says as he lets the door close.

"Better, I have a video." Sam says smiling.

"Nice job kid." Frank says as he steps up to watch as Samuel plays a ten second clip for him. The video shows a very well dressed elderly woman passing through the lobby with a man. She's tiny, probably five feet tall Frank estimates with snow white hair tied back in a tight bun. She walks erect and deliberate with graceful moves, like a dancer, her head held high. As Sam's video zooms in, Olivia Kinsey turns revealing cold, piercing, soul-stealing eyes that seem to penetrate the lens and with that, the video ends… her gaze gives Frank a slight chill.

"Sorry Mr. Elliot, I got a bit freaked out at the end, thought maybe she caught me." Sam says apologetically.

"No worries, do you mind Sam?" Frank says as he reaches for the phone and Sam willingly hands it over. Frank sits on the arm of the sofa and plays it again. Based on the little Frank gleamed from Willow's flash drive, Kinsey has to be at least a hundred years old, the woman in the video doesn't look anywhere near that. "Are you sure this is her?" He asks.

"Absolutely." Sam replies.

Frank plays it once more, now concentrating on the person accompanying Kinsey, a tall lean man dressed in a vintage cut chauffeur's outfit, his matching hat tucked under his arm as he walks. He has graying hair; clean cut with a square chin and dark penetrating eyes. He's older than Frank, probably seventy but moves like a panther, smooth, effortless and looks like he can hold his own. "Who's the guy?" Frank asks, freezing the video on the man as he turns the screen to Sam.

"His name is Wellington, not sure if that's a first or last name. He's Ms. Kinsey's personal driver, I've never seen her without him." Samuel answers.

"What about a security detail?" Frank asks.

Sam looks at him oddly.

"Sorry, I'd hate for some overly aggressive bodyguard to misinterpret my approach and dump me face down on the floor." Frank lies.

"Oh…yeah, I get that, no, not that I've ever seen." Samuel says. Frank hands him a fifty. Sam puts his hands up. "Hey, no Mr. Elliot, I can't take that. You paid me enough already."

"Take it kid, you made my life a lot easier." Frank replies smiling. "Seriously, just take it."

Sam shakes his head but grins and accepts the money.

"Get out of here." Frank says and Sam leaves. Frank plops on the couch, what the video revealed was not what he was expecting, Wellington looks dangerous and there's something downright eerie about Kinsey. Frank wonders what her role is in the big picture of things and, more importantly, who or…what the hell is she?

CHAPTER SIXTEEN

It's mid morning, as Frank slips on the jacket of his Italian made, navy blue, linen suit. He's taking his time, making sure he looks just right and moves to the mirror to inspect his reflection. He loves the feel of well fitted clothes and it's been awhile since he donned anything as comfortable as what he has on right now. They did a great job of tailoring, with the jacket sleeve showing just the right amount of shirt sleeve cuff and the break in the trouser legs is perfect. He refolds the silk pocket square before tucking it back into the jacket's breast pocket, adjusts the open collar of his shirt; he only wears ties for formal occasions and tucks a Smith & Wesson M&P compact automatic handgun in his back waistband. As he moves in to the hallway, he hangs a labeled laundry bag outside the door, which holds the much more casual clothes he arrived in, for cleaning. He takes the stairs down to the lobby, noticing that there are security cameras at the doors to each floor, exits at the lobby and nods to the front desk attendants as he passes. Frank moves with an air of confidence through the property that is accentuated even more so by his attire, he easily notices this by the glances from others as he passes, which is exactly the desired affect he wants. He's not trying to hide, he wants to blend in with the well heeled that patron this facility however, he still seems to be standing out from the crowd and he's okay with that too as he's well aware he is a bit vain. He enjoys a late brunch, modestly choosing from a crazy selection of everything under the sun accompanied by a few cups of rich Kona Peaberry coffee with its subtle hints of chocolate and buttery flavor. After, strolls the hotel investigating every public area he can and a few that he shouldn't but he needs to be as familiar with his surroundings as best he can, aware that with any hotel of this stature, there are security cameras strategically placed throughout and his actions may be scrutinized. He orders a tall glass of Perrier with a fresh lime wedge from the lounge and takes it along as he rides the elevator to the roof top terrace to get a better feel of the building's exterior layout and a bird's eye view of any strategic exit points he may need to take advantage of and takes the time to soak up the skyline views. He finally settles down in a corner of the lobby, which provides a clear view of the primary elevators and the main entrance, into a twilight patterned fabric chenille chair, orders a bottle of lime flavored Perrier to top off his glass and grabs a copy of the local paper, strategically placed on a midnight gold deco coffee table before him. His plan is too simply sit, watch and be as leisurely as he can about it. He trusts that if Kinsey knows him, it should be as a crew cut, clean shaven version of the bald headed and long bearded one here now. What he hopes to discover, he's not sure, that's what surveillance is all about, learning anything you can about your adversary even though she may not actually be one yet. It still bothers him, why, out of the blue, does the ex-head of the Committee want to meet him face to face? What is her end game, Christ…what is everyone's end game? Why he dwells on that, he's not sure, he has his own end game to worry about…never mind about everyone else. He's so engrossed in his thoughts that he almost misses Wellington walking through the lobby attired in his signature formal chauffeur's uniform. A charcoal grey double breasted jacket with a Chinese collar with two rows of silver buttons running down the front from each shoulder to the jacket's flap pockets, matching single pleated trousers and spit polish black dress shoes, his matching hat tucked under his arm as he walks, he does stand out. He leaves the hotel but quickly re-enters making his way to the elevator where he waits and momentarily a petite Ms. Olivia Kinsey exits the elevator, Versace sunglasses hide her icy penetrating eyes. Her white hair is still tied back in a bun and she's wearing an Albert contrast black and white checked coat with puffed polka dot faille sleeves, double breasted with exaggerated peak lapels, coordinated with Emanuelle checked silk blend trousers, black rock stud leather pumps and carrying a top-handle mini velvet and satin handbag. Frank is still taken back by her youthful appearance, not meaning she's young looking but she looks late seventies when she's supposedly closer to a hundred. His first thoughts, when he saw her in Sam's video, was that she was a Handler but that makes no sense considering she ruled the Committee with an iron fist but, on the other hand, that was Reggie's game plan. The pair head for the main entrance with Kinsey in the lead, neither looking in his direction as they move. As they exit Frank gets up, still holding the paper and makes his way to the center of the lobby to get a better view, checking for any additional security personnel that may have hung back inside. He watches from a distance as Kinsey and Wellington get in a metallic silver Rolls Royce Phantom and depart. He moves closer to the main doors looking for any sign of bodyguards outside but nothing there either. He's getting a feeling of déjà vu from when Zach drew him to the hotel in San Francisco where he openly displayed that he had no armed personnel protecting him inside. Is Kinsey pulling from the same play book, using Sherriff Barton as the sacrificial lamb to bring him here, draw him into a false sense of security and be brazen enough to try and take him out in broad daylight, in view of so many witnesses? He grips his automatic in his back waistband and turns in a slow circle, panning the room, searching for any hidden attackers and discovers none.

"Mr. Elliott, can I help you find something?" The front desk clerk asks as she approaches him; the same one that checked him in.

Frank stares at her a moment, releasing the hold on his weapon, letting his arm drop to his side. "No…I'm fine, just getting my senses stimulated by your entertaining décor." He finally answers.

She smiles. "I've never heard anyone describe it that way before."

"It's a compliment, I assure you." He says.

"Well, if you do need anything, please don't hesitate to ask." She says.

"Thank you." Frank replies, leaving her where she stands as he walks back to his half full glass of lime Perrier, picking it up as he drops the newspaper on the table and continues on into the lounge. His night is spent in his suite, electing to order room service again followed by a smoke on the balcony. He props his bare feet up on the railing as he enjoys his joint and watches, through the clear glass panels of the balcony railings, the social side of the city come alive with the setting sun and the end of the hustle and bustle of the business work day. The next two days were mundane ones for Frank; he learned little about Kinsey, as he only laid witness to a few trips in and out and little else but he knows he has to be patient and bide his time. Tonight, his fourth night here, is going to be different…he has a meet scheduled so he lounges on the balcony again, enjoying the sights and sounds to entertain himself until it's time for his rendezvous. Just before two a.m., as the streets below quiet down, Frank throws on the clothes he arrived at the Kompton in, black pants, t-shirt, a flight jacket and military boots and makes his way down a secondary stairway, out to a side street and sprints across to the back alley. He walks a hundred feet into the pitch black of the alley and stops. "Gaylord?" He loudly whispers.

"I am here." Gaylord announces as he steps out from the shadows.

"Wow!" Frank says with Gaylord's approach. "Is there something in the air or do you actually smell that good?"

Gaylord smiles. "I know humans do not care for the scent of us, they find it unpleasant so before I journey into their cities I always scrub myself in a stream with the fruit from Buffaloberry plants." He states.

"That must take a lot of berries." Frank laughs, coming in close and taking a strong whiff. "You smell like…strawberries."

"Do you find that pleasant?" Gaylord asks.

"Very pleasant." Frank replies chuckling as he steps back.

Gaylord grins.

"Follow me." Frank says and leads him near the alley entrance where he leans against a building wall to get a better view of the upper floors of the Kompton, Gaylord does the same. Frank points to his corner suite on the sixth floor that is facing their direction, the only room that is lit up. "See that place up there that has all the lights on?" Frank asks.

"I do." Gaylord replies without hesitation.

"Do you think you can make your way there without being seen?" Frank says.

Gaylord cautiously takes a couple steps closer to the lane to get a better perspective. "I can." He answers.

"Okay, I will go back and wave to you from my room just to confirm which one I'm in, I won't be able to see you in the dark but you'll see me just fine. After I signal you, I'll shut off the lights and wait for you." Frank says.

"I understand." Gaylord replies and steps further back into the dark of the alley.

Frank runs across the lane and slows to a walk as he nears 4th Avenue and the front of the Kompton, nods to the unknown doorman as he enters and heads to the elevators. Once in his room, he heads to the balcony, waves his arms to Gaylord in the alley below, shuts off the lights and waits. There's enough light coming through the open balcony door from the street to dimly light up the main living area. Frank has no idea how long it'll take Gaylord or how he's going to make his entrance but his questions are quickly answered by a sudden shudder as strong as a mild tremor that shakes the floor as Gaylord leaps onto the concrete floor of the balcony, catching Frank completely off guard.

Gaylord struts in, shrugging his shoulders. "It seemed the easiest and most direct way." He says.

Frank is a bit dumbfounded. "When you're right, you're right." He responds.

Eleven a.m. the next morning finds Frank parked in the lobby once more, reading the paper as he sips a Kona coffee. Earlier, after he double checked that he'd put out the "Do Not Disturb" door hanger, he had partaken in more of the scrumptious buffet the restaurant had to offer and patiently waited as his take out order of six large Waldorf salads and a dozen bottled water was readied for him… surprisingly his server never gave him a second look in regards to his request. He delivered it to Gaylord in the suite and promptly came back down to continue with his blasé surveillance of Kinsey and Wellington. An hour later, Wellington, still attired in his uniform, enters the lobby from the street and comes in his direction; Frank feigns attention in the newspaper with his approach. Wellington stops a couple feet away and waits patiently, finally Frank lowers the paper to meet Wellington's gaze.

"Mr. Smirnov, are you enjoying your stay?" Wellington asks in a husky monotone voice.

Frank is taken aback by Wellington referring to him by his true name.

"You seemed surprised? Don't be, Ms. Kinsey has been expecting you." Wellington states.

Frank folds the paper, lobs it onto the coffee table and says nothing.

"Ms. Kinsey thought you may be tiring of watching her from afar for these last few days and was inquiring if you would like to join her in the penthouse for dinner tonight? This way you and she could get to know each other better." Wellington says.

"Are you sure you have the correct party, that your assumption I'm…observing her is accurate?" Frank replies.

Wellington smiles, displaying perfectly straight, brilliantly white teeth. "Ms. Kinsey owns this fine establishment, has for quite some time now, a worthwhile investment she believes although she does not advertise that fact, prefers to let most believe she's a tenant. The numerous cameras installed throughout this property also feed to her premises so she can monitor all the activity…we have been monitoring you ever since your arrival." He says.

Frank remains seated and takes a drink of his lukewarm brew as he contemplates matters. "So why am I alive?" Frank asks.

Wellington chuckles. "Ms. Kinsey does not see you as a threat or an enemy, you are simply part of the equation?"

"What equation would that be?" Frank says.

"That is something you would need to discuss with her." Wellington says and hands Frank a swipe card. "You will need this to access the tenth floor from the elevator, Suite A."

Frank accepts it. "What time?"

"Is nine p.m. too late? Ms. Kinsey prefers to eat later in the evening, it helps her sleep." Wellington inquiries.

"Nine will be fine." Frank answers.

"I will advise Ms. Kinsey, enjoy the rest of your day." Wellington says with a nod of his head and walks away.

Part of the equation…could she actually be another rogue Handler? Frank watches as Wellington marches his way to the elevator, unsure of why he accepted Kinsey's invitation or what he'll be walking into tonight. His grandpa use to say "Don't mess with what you know nothing about"…screw it; it's time to break some rules.

CHAPTER SEVENTEEN

"My brother, are you certain you should do this?" Gaylord asks.

"Gaylord, just make sure you do as I've instructed, okay?" Frank replies as he finishes the shine on his black Bergamo shoes. He slips them on and walks back to the bedroom to put on his black Louis Vuitton suit jacket that just came back from the hotel's dry cleaning service. He's been sending out a suit and a shirt everyday to make sure he always has something fresh and clean considering he has such a limited wardrobe for his stay. He tucks a check patterned black and white silk pocket square in the breast pocket, adjusts the sleeves of his French cuff white dress shirt, straightening the cross style cuff-links as he examines himself in the mirror. He takes the Smith & Wesson automatic laying on the bed and places it in the night stand; he won't need a weapon tonight and walks back out to the living area to Gaylord. "We good about everything?"

"Yes." Gaylord answers.

Frank walks to the door, carefully opening it to make sure no one is passing that may spot Gaylord, makes sure the "Do Not Disturb" hanger is still in place and gives Gaylord a quick nod before exiting. He rides the elevator to the tenth floor and as the doors open, he finds himself facing the double entry doors to Suite A. He walks the hallway first and finds there's only one other suite on this floor and a sole exit to the stairway. As he heads back to Suite A, he waves to the security cameras in the ceiling, stops, opens his jacket, lifting it up around his chest and slowly turns in a circle. He then pulls up his pant legs as well to demonstrate he's not armed. He figures he'd save Wellington the inconvenience of patting him down. He takes the final few steps to Suite A, ignores the doorbell and knocks, noticing there's no peep holes in the doors. Momentarily, Wellington answers.

"Good evening Mr. Smirnov, please come in." He says.

Franks enters a suite much larger than his but is surprised that the décor is very similar, he had expected something more…opulent.

"Thank you for your display." Wellington says, referring to Frank's hallway exhibit. "It does make things less dramatic."

"I thought it may help in easing the tensions for tonight's meet." Frank replies.

"Of course, this way please." Wellington adds and leads Frank further in to the penthouse, to the dining area, where Olivia Kinsey is already seated at the table near the lit fireplace although it's a warm summer day.

She remains seated with his approach but extends out a hand to greet him. Her hair style remains unchanged and up close, her skin is smooth but so pale she almost looks like a corpse. She does look young for her age but at the same time, she appears ancient. She's wearing a Pakistani designed black chiffon long sleeved dress with an embroidered neckline and embellished with floral motifs throughout the front, gold piping is finished on the neck, sleeves and slits. "Mr. Smirnov, a pleasure to finally meet you." She says, her voice is husky and crisp.

Frank shakes her petite, bony hand with its long manicured black painted finger nails and it feels icy cold in his grip. "Please, call me Frank." He answers stepping back and resting his hands on the back of one of the dining chairs.

"Then you should call me Olivia." She says. "I hope you don't mind," Indicating to the covered platters on the white clothed table. "But I took the liberty of ordering for us."

"I'm sure your selection will be wonderful." Franks replies smiling.

"Good." She says. "Please have a seat."

"Allow me sir." Wellington interrupts, moving forward to pull the chair out for Frank.

Frank steps in front of it, as if to sit and while Wellington has a grasp of its back, he quickly spins hitting Wellington full force with a lethal knife-hand blow to the side of his throat. The strike collapses his carotid artery and can cause intense pain, unconsciousness due to the sudden and dangerous precipitous drop in blood pressure. In this case the damage is catastrophic and Wellington drops to the floor dead. Frank allows his eyes to go black and calmly moves around the chair to stand over the body, his eyes never leaving Olivia's as he places his foot on Wellington's throat and presses down with full force, slowly crushing it, the sound of splintering cartilage seems to echo in the still of the room.

Olivia displays no emotion but sighs. "I understand you wanted to make a point but I wish you hadn't done that…I actually liked him." She says, lifting an embroidered white cloth napkin from her lap, placing it on the table and taking a sip from the red liquid in the goblet in front of her. "Well, this is definitely not how I expected things to progress between us. I had hoped for…better."

"I'm glad to hear you can be surprised, that not everything goes as you trusted it should." Frank replies, letting his eyes return to normal as he takes a seat, interlocking the fingers of his hands and resting his forearms on his thighs. "Who… or should I ask, what are you and what do you want with me?"

"As you have experienced, no one is what they appear to be." She answers, with a hint of a smirk on her closed mouth.

Frank sighs and nods his acknowledgement. "Yea, too often. So…is this meet Committee sanctioned or are you going solo?"

Olivia smiles through thin red lips, displaying slightly crooked and yellowing teeth. "Because I once headed the Committee, does not necessarily mean my actions are in their best interests. It is a position which provided me with the power and influence to maintain my assigned agenda and it still does." She answers.

"And what exactly is that agenda?"

"It is one that is dictated by a higher power, you could say." She states smiling. Her eyes appear to light up with that statement.

"Are you a Handler?" Frank asks.

Olivia cackles. "No." She replies. "My role is just the opposite, to ensure that the heartaches, the suffering, the stress, the fear and the ultimate destruction continues for all. I am at my happiest, at my best when those around me are feeling dejected, lost with no sense of hope now or in the foreseeable future. I am here to ensure no one gets what they want, not humans, not the Handlers, not the Tsiatko maybe…not even you.

"How would you know what I want? I'm not even sure what that may be so how can you impede on what I don't even know?" Frank lies.

"I believe you already know that answer." She replies smiling. "Time repeating itself?"

Frank mulls over her words. "Are you the devil or it's representative?" Frank asks.

Olivia laughs and grabs the cloth napkin from the table to wipe a small drop of drool that is escaping her lips, leaving a smear of scarlet lipstick on its material and takes another drink from her glass. "You don't strike me as a religious man." She replies.

"I'm not."

"Then why would you use such a term?" She says.

"It seemed to be an appropriate label to use, nothing more." Frank answers.

"Yes…I guess it would, from your perspective."

"How long have you been here?" Frank says.

Olivia's eyes light up as she grins. "I have been on this world as long as the Tsiatko." She answers.

"Are you flesh and blood?" Frank asks.

"Yes." She replies. "The same as you…the same as most on this world."

Frank nods and smiles. "I was hoping that would be your answer." Frank says and with that Gaylord emerges from the next room and stands behind Frank. Unknown to Olivia, he's heard their entire conversation as Frank had instructed him to do and he isn't happy, his rage is clearly obvious by his glaring look, his bared teeth and the low grumble of a snarl escaping his throat.

"Olivia peers around Frank to get a better view. "Look at you." She says in a condescending tone, smirking. "You brought your furry friend but as Wellington already explained, you have nothing to fear from me, not yet anyways."

"He's not here for me, he's here for you." Frank states.

"I don't understand." Olivia replies, cocking her head.

"I hoped that would be your answer." Frank says as he crosses his arms on his chest and leans back slightly in his chair. "I have learned much more from the Orb than I believe anyone expected, even about you and your intentions." Frank replies offering no other details. "So when good old Sherriff Barton approached me about our meeting, my first instinct was that it was time to get my hands dirty, I wanted blood…I mean, I got his but I wanted yours too. Instead I decided there was a better route to go, to let the Tsiatko know the true you and let them deal with your fate.

There is a look of fright on Kinsey's face. She suddenly suspects what's coming next and it was not part of the equation. "Wait…you can't be serious?!" She exclaims.

Gaylord," Frank instructs. "She's all yours."

Before Olivia can scream, Gaylord leaps forward and clamps his huge hand on her head, covering her face, muffling her cries, her skull buried in his grip like a baseball. He drags her, like a small rag doll, from the chair into the living area and suspends her in the air by her head and takes his time tearing her apart, limb by limb so she can experience as much of the excruciating pain as possible before the life drains from her. Frank doesn't move, stays seated nor does he look away, he remains emotionless at the sight of the bloody carnage. It's over in a couple of minutes but Frank hopes it seemed like a lifetime to her. Gaylord drops her white haired skull; nothing else is left attached, to the floor moving his head back and forth like he's working out a kink in his neck as he surveys Olivia's tattered remains. Frank gets up and moves to the door.

"Brother, where are you going?" Gaylord calls out.

Frank opens the door and looks back. "I have to go, there's something I need to finish." He answers.

"When will I see you again?" Gaylord asks.

"I'm not sure." Frank replies, closing the door behind him. He heads back to his room, packs and calls the front desk.

"How can we help you tonight Mr. Elliott?" The desk clerk answers.

"Is Sam working?" Frank asks.

"He is." Is the reply.

"Can you send him up to my room, I'm checking out." Frank says.

"Do you need a receipt for your stay?" The attendant asks.

"No, I'm good." Frank answers.

"Thank you for your business Mr. Elliott and we hope to have you back one day soon. Sam will be up shortly."

Frank walks out on the balcony and leans on the railing to wait, taking in the sounds, the sights along with the pleasant smell of the salty waters from the nearby bay, wondering what will become of all of this. His thoughts are interrupted by the doorbell and he lets Sam in.

"Sorry to hear you're leaving." Sam says.

"Well, my meeting with Ms. Kinsey went better than I expected." He answers.

"Good to hear." Sam replies as he loads everything on the luggage cart.

Frank grabs the sports bag holding the Orb off the top of the pile. "I'll take this one."

"You're the boss." Sam says, heading for the door. They ride the elevator down in silence and Sam leads the way to Frank's waiting Mercedes. Frank places the sports bag behind his seat and leans on the roof and watches Sam loads the trunk. Task done, he closes it. "All yours Mr. Elliot, drive safe."

"Here." Frank says, tossing Sam a packet of hundred dollar bills.

Sam catches it, quickly examining the stack of one hundred dollar bills. "What the fuck?!" He exclaims.

"Enjoy life while you can kid, you never know how long you've got in this world." Frank says smiling as he climbs in, starting the powerful V8 turbo engine and speeding off, laying a streak of rubber before Sam can even reply.

Its morning and Frank is enjoying the views on this final leg to Mt. Rainier, unsure if this will be his last time. The walls of tall fir and pine trees he's in between makes the road look so narrow, as if they're going to engulf him. He follows the curve and these same trees dwarf and almost disappears, overshadowed by the mountains that springs into view. The Mercedes hugs the highway as he rounds another turn, the route's appearance changes again to one of a steep hillside comprised of stick-like trees on one side, the opposite side transforms into a deep gully of fir and pine blended with an array of alder, cedar, hemlock and yew. The sight still gives him an ominous feeling, like the roadster is going to slip off the edge into the valley below and he'll never to be seen again…maybe, that would be for the best. He relishes the way the morning sun lights up these surroundings and this landscape, how these mountains and valleys becomes a sea of green. He loves that this laneway through nature is this simple straight roadway and then becomes this serpentine of a path that weaves an umpteen track of long slow curves and sudden sharp turns. He's enjoying the drive even though he's been on it countless of times, he still hasn't tired of it. This highway is still impressive, the curves smooth and seamless, no potholes, no irregularities. He likes this roadway; it inspirits him and he slows as he approaches the Mt. Rainier National Park's parking lot once more.

EPILOGUE

Frank reaches the highest summit of Mt. Rainier, Columbia Crest; fourteen thousand four hundred feet above sea level. It's taken little effort for him to climb the mountain this time compared to when he and Zach did, in the cold of winter when they were in search of the caverns hidden below Rainier's summit, in search of the Tsiatko and the Orb. The trek has only taken him two days as he didn't need any down time to acclimatize. On the first day he made it all the way to Camp Muir, stayed overnight in the public shelter and then continued on. He wasn't weighed down this time with a hundred and ten pound pack as he only required some water and a few rations, all because of the Orb.

He's returned to where his adventure began. His enlightenment. His destiny. That is the key word…his. And now, he will have his redemption. He sets down his knapsack and unpacks the Orb and stands to survey the world before him on this sunny, clear day. It seems, he's truly at the top of the world. He's mesmerized by the view, maybe more so now, as he wonders if the landscape will change. He soaks up the beauty that lies before him in every direction as there are no clouds so he can see out for a hundred miles with Mt. Adams and Mt. Hood in the horizon. His mind drifts thinking about the past and what all could have been on this world he now accepts and calls home.

He's lost, entranced in his thoughts and he has become oblivious to his surroundings, they've faded away. He's gone for seconds, minutes…maybe an hour but is brought back to reality by what sounds like millions of small feet gently shuffling along a beach of soft dry sand. He looks down and around. Every open piece of ground, as far as he can see is filled with a never ending ocean of Tardigrades…Water Bears. They've surrounded him but halt their progress, stopping as a single entity a few feet away. He can feel the strong mountain winds on his face but their sound is drowned out by a continuous whirring thrumming song now emitting from this sea of hungry creatures. It's as if these beasts have appeared out of nowhere and in a sense they have, as Frank gently rolls the Orb from one hand to the other pondering their arrival. One of these strange animals comes semi-shuffling towards him. This once microscopic being is now the size of a medium dog and looks like a cross between a Shar-Pei and a caterpillar. Its puckered body has eight wrinkly short legs and each limb has a half dozen evil looking claws protruding from the end of it. Its eyes are tiny round black dots the size of a pea and it has a big rumpled snout of a mouth…if it can even be called a mouth as it looks more like an extended suction cup. Scientists first discovered them on this planet in the seventeen seventies and have theorized they're an alien life form that can withstand virtually anything, extreme heat; bitter cold and they can go without food or water for years. It is theorized that they can withstand radiation hundreds of times higher than what would be lethal to humans, survive an asteroid impact, even live in outer space and its speculated there are untold millions of them on this planet. Frank knows this is all true, that they have all these capabilities and they are alien, just like mankind here is. The Handlers brought them from Mars as well but left them in a microscopic state to render them harmless. Frank discovered a means through the Orb, to restore them to their original size. He squats down and gently pets the one at his feet and he's still amazed how soft it is. It looks like it's covered in bare skin but it has a plushy silky feel to it. The strange whirring thrum sound is it purring, like a cat and it begins to rub itself against Frank's thigh, its snout pointed upward. Frank laughs. Their snouts are tough to remove once they latch on. Water Bears live only on fluids and considering humans are about seventy percent fluids; they'd suck a human dry in four to five minutes. He faces no harm from them as he's their Master and he's trained them for a specific purpose. Frank stands and gazes around at the mass of Water Bears as he tenderly strokes the Orb. "Don't worry my beauties; you'll all feed to your heart's content very soon." He gently speaks out to them, knowing they understand every word he's saying. He takes a step forward. "They're coming!! "He yells out to the world. "Coming for all of you, every single bastard one of you, whoever and whatever you are!! This world WILL be cleansed once more but," He grins with anticipation. "It WILL be done my way this time!! You hear me?!! My way!!" And he turns away quickly, as if attempting to ignore the populations' phantom pleas to stop. He plops down on the hard, rocky terrain and brings his knees up to prop the blue hued Orb on them and he gently raps his forehead against its surface. He closes his eyes, let's himself breathe and calm down. The purring of the Water Bears is soothing and he feels their whirring whispering gently vibrate through his body, like a relaxing massage. His feels his body sag and droop as the tension escapes, something it hasn't done in so, so long and he sits, enjoying the sensation…breath in…breath out…breath in…breath out.

Who is he to be judge and jury as he recounts those emotions he first felt when he discovered, through the very object he's now holding, the immense human loss at the hands of the Handlers but he's not the Frank he use to be back then even though that was such a short time ago. Maybe he should disappear and leave the Tsiatko and humans to battle it out. With Kinsey's death, he has cleared a major hurdle for the Tsiatko and if they go to war and win, where does he fit in? He cannot see himself living among them nor does he feel part of the human race. He's at a loss…maybe…maybe Mr. H's warning was meant only for Frank, to trust no one other than himself? To do what he feels is right for this lost planet with no future? He finally looks out at the world before him and finds that the Water Bears are gone so he stands and makes his way down the slope. He pauses after only traveling a hundred feet. "Shit." He says turning back towards the summit. As he slowly walks back up the rocky, loose terrain, the sound of his boot steps crunching on the surface below is soon drowned out by the ever increasing thrumming of Water Bears. "Fuck em." Frank announces as he reaches the peak. "I will play God."

THE XENO MANIFESTO

THE XENO MANIFESTO – RECLAMATION

THE XENO MANIFESTO – REDEMPTION

Website – www.brysenmann.com
Instagram – brysenmann
Twitter - @brysen_mann
Facebook - @brysenmann